MILLS

Centenary Collection

Celebrating 100 years of romance with the very best of Mills & Boon

All the characters in this book have no existence outside the
imagination of the author, and have no relation whatsoever to anyone
bearing the same name or names. They are not even distantly inspired
by any individual known or unknown to the author, and all the
incidents are pure invention.

First published in Great Britain 2008
by Harlequin Mills & Boon Limited,
Eton House, 18-24 Paradise Road, Richmond, Surrey TW9 1SR

ISBN: 978 0 263 86640 7

76-0508

Harlequin Mills & Boon policy is to use papers that are
natural, renewable and recyclable products and made from
wood grown in sustainable forests. The logging and
manufacturing processes conform to the legal environmental
regulations of the country of origin.

Printed and bound in Spain
by Litografia Rosés S.A., Barcelona

The Man From Southern Cross

by

Margaret Way

MILLS & BOON®

Pure reading pleasure

Margaret Way takes great pleasure in her work and works hard at her pleasure. She enjoys tearing off to the beach with her family at weekends, loves haunting galleries and auctions and is completely given over to French champagne 'for every possible joyous occasion'. She was born and educated in the river city of Brisbane, Australia, and now lives within sight and sound of beautiful Moreton Bay.

Chapter One

HE LEFT the mustering camp late afternoon, when the still-blazing sun was slipping down the sky in a glory of red, gold and amethyst.

Every bone, every muscle in his body was throbbing with fatigue. It had been a long hard day made doubly frustrating because he and a handful of the men had to fight yet another brushfire at the old "dancing grounds."

The aboriginals claimed, perhaps with perfect truth, that the grounds were sacred and the brushfires, which had gone on for as long as anyone could remember, were the work of Jumboona, one of the more mischievous of the ancient gods. Sometimes when he was tired, like now, he accepted that possibility with a laconic shrug. Unless the fires were lit deliberately—and no one had ever found any evidence of it—there seemed to be no easy explanation. As his father used to say, "Old Jumboona strikes again!" Charlie Eagle-hawk, their best tracker, claimed to have seen Jumboona through the flames, but then Charlie specialized in stories that made the hair on the back of one's neck prickle.

He rode on, allowing the splendor of the sunset to revive him. The muster would resume at dawn the next day, but there was a tension in the men and in the cattle he didn't much like. The hot winds had a bearing on it. As well, for the aboriginal stockmen, Jandra Crossing was the site of an old ritual killing by one of the dreaded *kurdaitcha* men, dispensers of justice since the Dreamtime. Stories about the ritual *kurdaitcha* killings were interwoven with the legends of Southern Cross; so were the stories about Jumboona and his hostile cavortings. Jumboona certainly liked to keep them all busy, he thought now with a sort of rueful humor.

A wallaby jumped out in front of his big stallion, The Brigadier, who executed a high-stepping dance. He reined the horse in, then pushed his akubra farther back on his head, looking up at the sky. It was pearlescent with smoke, the smell of burned bush land hot in his nostrils. Even the birds seemed disturbed, sending up spine-tingling shrieks as they flew home to the billabongs and swamps. The *kurdaitcha* man's victims, transgressors of the tribal laws, were said to wander the lignum swamps at night. Many a stockman over the long years had claimed to see their spirits setting up camp near the water. He had never seen anything paranormal himself, and he didn't expect to. But even his so-called iron nerves had been tested now and again in the hill country, where the extensive network of caves served as immensely old galleries for images of love magic and sorcery.

Southern Cross, the Mountford desert stronghold since

the 1860s, was also a mythical place for the Jurra Jurra tribe. So the legends had begun and were allowed to grow. This was his country and he loved it with a passion. No woman could ever hold him in the same way. At thirty, with half a dozen affairs behind him, he had reason to know. He'd come close to marriage once—it was expected that at some stage he would provide the historic Mountford station with an heir—but he'd found himself unable to take the final step. No woman had ever fired his blood.

Dusk saw him riding through the main compound on his way to the huge complex of stables at the rear of the homestead. He dismounted in the circular courtyard, looking around. Where the hell was Manny? Probably whittling away at one of his little wooden sculptures; they were so good, he thought it was about time he encouraged the boy to do something with his skill. He summoned him with a loud whistle and Manny came running, his face split in a wide grin.

"Old Jumboona get yah again, Boss?"

Tired as he was, he couldn't help returning Manny's infectious grin. "The worst thing, Manny, is that you seem to enjoy it."

"No, Boss." Manny shook his curly head. "You'll cut 'im down to size and that's a fact. I'm beginnin' to wonder if the old boy ain't losin' his powers."

His laugh rasped in his dry throat. "You should have spent the day with me. And I wouldn't speak too loudly, either. The old boy might hear you."

"Wouldn't bother about the likes o' me." Manny took

charge of The Brigadier's saddle. "Saw Miss Annabel a while ago. She was all excited about her friend."

Her friend! God, he didn't know whether to laugh or bang his head against the stone wall. He'd clean forgotten about Annabel's friend. She would be up at the homestead right now.

"Everything okay, Boss?" Manny asked anxiously.

"I just need an ice-cold beer, Manny. And a hot tub. In that order." He didn't say the thought of having to make small talk with a strange woman intensified his feelings of tiredness and irritation. He swept off his akubra and ran an impatient hand through his hair, black and shiny as a magpie's wing. It was too thick and too long at the back and, he supposed, that together with the marks of grime and smoke gave him the appearance of a wild man. Not exactly what Miss Roishin—what kind of name was that?—Grant would expect to see. He laughed out loud remembering how some women's magazine had voted him one of the sexiest men in the country. Eligible and rich. The *rich* surely helped; the *sexy* bit amazed him. He knew he was attractive to women, but he didn't flatter himself unduly. Most women were very frivolous, he'd found. They had this big ongoing affair with glamour and glitz.

His thoughts inevitably shifted to the wedding. In a few days' time, Annabel, his stepsister—the elder, by fully five minutes, of identical twins—was to be married in the homestead's ballroom, with the reception in the Great Hall. The whole thing had gotten a little out of hand as far as he was concerned. And he was footing the bill.

To be fair, as a leading "landed" family, their guest list had to be long. The extended Mountford family was spread over three states, with Southern Cross the ancestral home. They all expected to be represented, along with close friends, business friends, the usual socialites, assorted politicians and a fair sprinkling of the legal profession to which the groom, Michael Courtney, belonged. It sometimes seemed to him that half the country had been invited, but Annabel assured him 250 guests was the lowest possible count. Roishin—was it Gallic for rose?—was one of the four bridesmaids. She had been a close friend of the twins at university, yet strangely enough he had never met her. The one time she'd visited the station he'd been on a business trip to Texas, seeing a fellow rancher. The girls, Annabel and Vanessa, spent a lot of time with her in Sydney where she lived and he maintained an apartment as a family pied-à-terre. When he'd had time to listen, he'd learned that her father was a merchant banker, her mother a divorce lawyer. Roishin probably arranged flowers. The twins, "the Mountford heiresses" as they were usually referred to in the press, didn't work much, either. He, as head of the Mountford clan since the untimely death of his father, worked like a dog and always had.

His stepmother, Sasha, of whom he was very fond, had taken to spending a good deal of her time traveling. In fact, Sasha's travels had become something of a family joke. His own mother, Charlotte, had walked out on him and his father after a grueling seven years of marital war. His father had applied for custody of their only child, with the considerable weight of the family's power and influence behind him, and had emerged triumphant, just as everyone had known he would. *He* had been the heir, the helpless six-year-old victim who'd never been prepared for the emotional devastation. Even now, sometimes, in some deep place inside him, it hurt like hell. He'd had such love for his mother. Enormous love. He'd worshiped her. For years he just couldn't take in her treachery. She had left them both for a man she hadn't even bothered to marry.

His father had engineered it so that he rarely saw his mother. On those few occasions, he'd been full of hurt and hostility, very difficult to handle. He hadn't seen his mother in many years now, though Sasha persisted in trying to shove photographs in the glossies under his nose. She was Lady Vandenberg now, wife of Eric Vandenberg, the industrialist. His mother had tried to make contact with him after his father's death, but feeling as he did, he couldn't bring himself to see her. *She* was the one who had made an art form of rejection.

He decided to enter the house through the front door. It was the quickest route upstairs, where he had the entire west wing to himself. Sasha and the twins shared the east wing. The house was so big they could all rattle around in it without even seeing each other. The Hon. George Clifford Mountford had begun work in the early 1860s on what was to become a thirty-five room mansion. The complex of surrounding buildings included a picturesque old stone church built for the master, his family and servants. No way could it accommodate 250 wedding guests, but the big reception rooms at the homestead could.

He had barely moved across the threshold when the sound of footsteps along the gallery made him look up. A young woman was descending the staircase at a rush.

His first thought was she had strayed out of a painting. Something by John Singer Sargent. Her image stamped itself indelibly on his mind. She was a waking dream, a creature of incredible light and grace. She kept moving… floating…. Colors shimmered. She had long dark hair with a burnish of purple, luminous white skin, large faintly slanted blue or green eyes. He couldn't be sure. Her full mouth, so fresh and tender, was smiling in some kind of pleasurable anticipation. She was wearing what had to be her brides-maid's gown. A sumptuous champagne silk creation with a neckline cut to reveal bare sloping shoulders. The rich material gleamed. The beading and embroidery on the bodice and the full sleeves flickered and flashed in the light from the chandelier. She was tantalizing…tantalizing….

Something like a wave of heat broke over him. It was as though his skin caught fire. Just as he thought no woman could move him, he felt a shock of desire so powerful his fists clenched instinctively until the knuckles showed white. For an instant he was the helpless male again. Bitter and powerless in the face of a woman's sheer magic. He was no match for her. The thought appalled him, influenc-ing his attitude drastically.

She looked down. Saw him. Became arrested, unsure of her next movement. She'd been hurrying down the staircase, one hand holding up the skirt of her long billowing gown, the other trailing along the banister. Now she stood immobilized.

Adrenaline pumped through him, energizing his tired body and keying up his senses. Experience had taught him to be a very careful man. But here she was! Out of nowhere, a crisis in his life. And more than anything he wanted her away. Back to the city and the hothouse where she belonged. Such women couldn't bloom in the desert. They only brought heartbreak and trouble.

He saw her make a visible effort to speak. A soft ripple moved her throat. "You must be David. We've never met, have we? How do you do? I'm Roishin."

She had a lovely voice, warmly pitched, self-possessed. Or it would have been except for the faintest tremor. Perhaps his appearance frightened her? The wild hair, the dark stubble of beard, his stained clothes. She pronounced her name Roh-sheen with the accent on the second syllable. Appropriately, it sounded like a name from myth and legend.

Any civilized man would have moved to greet her, but he stood perfectly still, making her come to him. No one had ever called him David except his mother. He'd been Mont to his father, as he was to Sasha and the twins. Mountford to just about everyone else, including family.

She went to give him her slender white hand, but he evinced cool surprise. "Welcome to Southern Cross," he said, aware his voice sounded curt and formal. "I won't take your hand. I'm covered in grime and it's important not to mark your beautiful gown."

There was a fraught little silence as if she realized he didn't want to touch her. Her iridescent eyes darkened, glistened as though stung by tears.

I want her, he thought. *This is the woman who will change my life.*

Chapter Two

HE KNEW he was quiet at dinner. Once or twice he caught Sasha and the twins looking at him, obviously wondering why he wasn't making his usual contribution to the conversation, especially when a guest was present. But Roishin Grant was having a strange effect on him. She might have been a creature from another planet, beguiling his eye but stilling his tongue. Her presence undermined his control, dredging up some part of him he'd thought long buried—a need and a longing that seemed to possess him although he was reluctant to experience such emotions again. Remembered love burned in him. For an instant he had a clear recollection of his mother sitting where Sasha was sitting now. He wasn't aware of it, but his eyes turned stormy. The pain had dulled, but not the anger. The anger was a permanent scar.

His mother had been beautiful in just the way this woman was beautiful. Dark-haired, jewel-eyed, pale-skinned. Bewitching, where Sasha and the twins with their fair pretty faces and rounded curves had the freshness of apples. Tonight she wore something silky in a swirl of blues, greens and purples, the V neckline allowing tantalizing glimpses of the shadowy cleft between her breasts. Her features in the rose gold lighting had the perfection of sculpture, but the eyes and the mouth were ravishingly female. That he could do without. He could even understand why a man might want to marry a sensible plainfaced woman. A *dull* woman, who wouldn't have the capacity to inflict mortal wounds.

From time to time, because he couldn't resist it, he inserted a probing question, which she parried without fluster. She had a charming candid way about her, but he was determined to remain unimpressed—far from easy when his every sense was being seduced. By the time coffee arrived, the realization suddenly hit him that *she* had been drawing *him* out. And she'd done it with considerable tact and skill, leaving him in no doubt that as a lawyer she'd be a very deft operator. In a whispered aside, Annabel had told him about Roishin's qualification in law. Another shock. Not a flower-arranging dilettante, after all. At least she had a career to take her straight back home. She wouldn't be lingering here to finish what she'd started—the oldest story in the world. Seduction.

He excused himself fairly early, saying he had correspondence to attend to; it was true, but had their guest been almost anyone else, the job would have kept. Later, when he was drafting a letter to the chairman of a government committee of which he was a member, he heard them fooling around the piano. Both his sisters played, Annabel extremely well, and he smiled to himself as she launched into a spirited and highly embellished version of Mendelssohn's "Wedding March." It was so entertaining he got up to open his door. From "The Wedding March," Annabel began to work her way through a number of songs, old and new, love songs, wedding songs, with Vanessa singing snatches as her twin played. Sasha, who wasn't terribly accurate with her pitching, called for an old wedding song that had probably been all the rage in her day and began singing it almost before Annabel had finished the introduction.

He put down his pen, listening to the words.

His own lips formed the words ironically. *Promise me.* Promises. Love and togetherness…

His mother had made sacred promises she had never kept. She had scorned the husband she'd married in the sight of God, abandoned her small son. So much for promises and dazzling women. He had a sure instinct in these matters.

Sasha was having difficulties with her vocalizing, and another voice took over. At first happily, slightly exaggerating the sentimental lyrics, then as though with a sudden change of heart, seriously, in a voice that held him spellbound.

His hands on the huge mahogany partner's desk, his father's desk, clenched and unclenched. He'd *liked* Vanessa's version of some Whitney Houston song, but this was unbearably sweet, a naturally beautiful female voice singing an old song with great tenderness, sincerity and purity. Annabel's accompaniment moved into a matching mode, became stirring, full of feeling. The extreme top note soared with ease and absolute certainty. As a performance it was unique in his experience, invading caverns in his heart he had thought sealed.

Annabel called a spontaneous "Bravo!", clapping like a devotee at a classical concert.

Vanessa, as always, seconded her, barely a heartbeat later, sounding the least bit tearful. Then Sasha's astonished, "That was *lovely,* Roishin!"

Now he heard *her* laugh. A melodious ripple, with a music all its own. He should have known from the cadences of her speaking voice that she could sing. Roishin Grant was becoming more disturbing by the minute.

Later he came to stand in the doorway to say goodnight. "I enjoyed the concert, ladies!" He gave a slight bow, contemplating the charming tableau, faces turned toward him. "Roishin was the soloist?" As though he didn't know.

"Yes, isn't she brilliant?" Pleasure and animation was all over Annabel's sunny open face. "She even made us cry."

"Dare I admit to a tear myself?" His eyes singled out Roishin briefly. He meant his tone to be pleasant, but even then an edge crept in. "Would you care to go riding in the morning, Roishin?" he asked, to make amends. What in sweet hell was making him say her name like that? It was rolling off his tongue like honey.

"Yes, go!" the others urged.

"You *do* ride?" Again the degree of challenge.

The twins exchanged glances, but Roishin was perfectly poised, looking at him with her iridescent eyes. Blue, green, he wasn't sure. They seemed to change dramatically with different flashes of color from her dress.

"I do, but I think as a renowned horseman and polo player you might judge me harshly."

"Mont's always kind to beginners," Van, his faithful disciple, said.

"Roishin doesn't look terribly convinced," Annabel laughed.

"I'd love to come with you, David." She smiled, softening his mood and charming him. "If it makes you feel happier, I belonged to a pony club as a child."

Her voice was actually connecting with his nerve ends, vastly unsettling him. "Well, that's something, I'm sure. Until the morning, then. Just around daybreak is perfect, but I suppose that's too early for you?" Did he have to make everything sound like a rebuke?

"Dawn sounds perfect." She continued to smile gently, humoring his abrasiveness. Her mouth was full, soft, with a pronounced cupid's bow. Was that supposed to mean sensuality? Vulnerability? All he knew was that he wanted to crush it with his own.

"We'll have breakfast waiting when you come home," Sasha promised, her smile registering a certain roguishness.

Don't try your matchmaking on me, Sasha, he thought. Fond as he was of his stepmother, he was the master of his own fate. And he had rejected Roishin Grant on sight.

HE AWOKE at first light from long habit, finding in himself an excitement he wanted to shut out. Damn and blast, what was the matter with him? He wasn't a callow adolescent. If he wanted to brag, he could have said he was immensely successful with women. But this Roishin Grant was affecting him sharply, bringing out something almost primitive in his nature. He felt threatened, hostile, enslaved. All at the same time. He couldn't help feeling a certain contempt for himself, as well. No woman was going to dominate his life ever again. He'd decided that long ago.

Still, the coming of Sasha, then the twins, had made Southern Cross cheerful. When he married—and he *would* have to—he'd have the sense to find an honest openhearted woman like Sasha. She'd brought peace, but no drama. His father's experience, and he remembered his beloved father in all his moods, had warned him off drama for life.

Yet here he was, showering and dressing at full speed. It was a spell of sorts, and he despised it. He scooped up his akubra and went out the door, hoping she'd have the sense to bring a hat. The sun would be up soon enough, and he found himself hating the thought of any burning to her skin. No wonder they described a woman's skin as "magnolia." Hers had the same flawless, creamy, stroke-me quality.

Miracle of miracles, she was waiting for him in the hallway, as straight as a boy except for the soft, high thrust of her breasts. She actually jumped when he came up behind her saying, "Hello, there," then swung to face him, her long hair, very thick and straight, brushed back from her face and caught in some kind of knot on her nape. As a hairstyle it couldn't have been more severe, but she carried it beautifully. In fact, he saw more this way—the lovely line of her jaw, the way it merged with the graceful column of her neck, the almost flower-like set of her ears.

"David, you startled me!" she gasped. "You have a very quiet tread."

"So I've been told." He could see a trace of something—near-fright?—in her eyes. "I'm sorry. I had no intention of alarming you." But she *knew* there was a hardness in him; a hardness that might make a sensitive woman shrink. "I'm glad you thought to bring a hat."

"One of Van's."

"Then put it on. The sun's strong even this early, and your skin is very white." He couldn't seem to keep his eyes off her, although that wasn't what he wanted at all. Her hair, her face, the feminine slope of her shoulders. She, too, stood staring up at him, like a creature trying to struggle out of a trap.

"I'm not arguing with you, David," she said finally, putting the hat on and adjusting the chin strap. "It's very obvious that you're right—and it's equally obvious that you're accustomed to command."

His gaze raked her, trying to decipher her expression. "I *do* run Southern Cross. And I know that any other way wouldn't work." He extended his arm, indicating she should precede him out the door.

Manny was already up and about, parading his infectious grin. "Mornin' Boss. Mornin' Miss."

"Miss Grant," he told the boy briefly.

"Miss Grant, o'course!" Manny studied Roishin with immense approval.

"Good morning, Manny," she smiled. "We've met before. Don't you remember?"

"Sure do, ma'am. Are you gonna take the same horse?"

"And which horse was that?" Mountford asked, deceptively quiet.

"Miss Grant's a plenty good rider," Manny told him warmly. "She really knows how to treat horses."

"That doesn't exactly answer my question, Manny."

"She took The Brigadier!" Manny whooped.

He looked and felt thoroughly jolted. "The Brigadier is much too strong for a woman."

Manny sobered abruptly, doing a little mime with his hands.

"Please don't blame Manny," Roishin begged. "I... rather insisted."

"Manny should know better. You won't be riding The Brigadier today." He couldn't control the curtness and he saw her flush. Damn! He didn't really want to upset her.

He gave an order to Manny and the boy moved away, returning a few moments later leading Star Lady, a small but beautifully proportioned silver gray mare with a sweet temper and a surprisingly long stride.

"Oh, isn't she lovely? Is she for me?" Roishin must have forgiven him, because she looked up at him with a smile that would have melted a stonier heart than his.

"She is. You'll find her a pleasant ride. I'll take The Brigadier...if you don't mind."

It didn't take long to saddle up the horses, and soon they were on their way. He rode the big, dashing jet black stallion that stood a good seventeen hands high. If she could hold The Brigadier as she must have done, she was an excellent horsewoman.

As he soon found out. The talk of the pony club had been no more than a tease. She was an experienced rider, with considerable style. A feeling of great contentment welled up in him, calming his inner conflicts. It was an incomparable feeling, riding together in the pearly dawn. The air was blissfully pure and cool, laden with the sweet scents of the bush. Bird song poured from the trees that scattered blossom like confetti as they rode beneath them and out onto the open plain. Her face beneath his sister's white akubra was alive with quick feelings. She looked entranced, as though the magic he always felt was getting to her, too. It pleased him more than he would ever have believed.

Not everyone understood the outback, its vastness and savage majesty. Some found it eerie, others intimidating, and many professed to a kind of atavistic fear that raised the short hairs on the backs of their necks. It had something to do with the enormous empty distances, the great silence, the play of color, light and shadow on the monumental primeval rocks. The outback had an incredible mystique. It was the wild beating heart of the most ancient continent on earth.

At one of the crystal-clear gullies overhung by the weeping casuarinas they came upon a small party of aboriginal women and children gathering herbs, and they exchanged greetings before moving on. After a long and agonizing drought, Southern Cross had experienced its first good season in years, and the wildflowers were prodigious, running in a marvelous multicolored embroidered carpet to the curiously domed hillocks that rose like Persian minarets on the station's western border.

At this time of day the hills were a soft pink, but like many of the great rocks of the interior they changed color with weather conditions, aspect and time of day. Mountford had seen them run the gamut from salmon pink to rose to glowing furnace red, then back to deep purple and misty mauve. There were aboriginal legends connected to every natural feature on the station, and as they slowed their exhilarating gallop to a comfortable walk, he began to point out different places of geographical interest, outlining the Dreamtime legends that went along with them.

The sun was up now in full splendor, dispersing the strange mists that hung like clouds along the ancient watercourses. The aborigines looked on them as guardian spirits, and to an imaginative eye they appeared to be just that, lying in milky circlets and ribbons only a few inches above the green canopy of trees. One could expect mists when a chill hung over the bush, but the mists moved in faithfully even when the weather was brilliantly clear and hot.

"Magic!" she said, listening to him. "And why not, in such a place?"

Her answer delighted him, but he tried to hide it. "Time to go back," he announced matter-of-factly, unwilling to prolong his joy in her company. "As Manny said, you know how to treat horses."

"Because they're such beautiful creatures!" She leaned forward to stroke the mare's neck. The wind had torn at her hair, releasing a few strands, which she casually brushed away. She turned her head to him, using one hand to shield her eyes from the strong slanting sunlight. "I *can* ride The Brigadier, you know."

"I'm sure you can, but I'd rather you didn't." He heard his own voice, deep, smooth, vaguely taunting. "I wouldn't care to see you break your lovely neck."

For all her poise, she flushed, a soft peach bloom on her cheeks. "You don't like me, do you, David?"

"What am I supposed to say to that?" He was surprised by her directness.

"Perhaps what you've got against me?"

"What idiotic nonsense!"

"Don't you realize how hostile you are?"

"Hostile, possibly," he agreed. "You disturb me, Miss Grant. You're…extremely direct. Anyway, it's nothing personal." Despite himself, he tried to explain. "Something about exotic creatures makes me tense inside."

"How? In what way?"

He glanced at her briefly, a silver sparkle in his eyes. "One can see you're a lawyer from all the practiced questioning. Surely you're not attempting to *analyze* me?"

"Forgive me. I'm just trying to understand what I've done. Annabel and Vanessa are my dear friends. I want you to like me."

"Presumably every man you meet *likes* you?" His tone was cool to the point of cutting—and there was nothing he could do about it.

"Well, I don't go around blazing out challenge."

"Don't you?"

"I want to be your friend, David. Please believe me."

"I'm sorry, Roishin." He smiled at her. "That may never happen."

FOR THE REST of the day he lost himself in backbreaking work, only returning to the house as the sun was setting in a blaze of varied reds and golds. He went straight to his room. Suite of rooms really—a bedroom the size of a football field, as Van described it, bathroom, dressing room, a sitting room large enough to accommodate some excellent pieces he had appropriated from other parts of the house. He was entirely self-contained and private, which was the way he liked it. One of these days he would have his wing of the house refurbished, but it all cost money. Big money. Much as he loved his ancestral home, he had to admit that its maintenance had created a few problems over the years. As well, he had outlaid an astonishing amount of money to have decorators flown in to pretty up the main reception rooms for the wedding. He intended to do Annabel proud. Vanessa, too, when it came her turn to be married. Whatever his fears of the femme fatales of this world, he understood that Sasha and his sisters were the sort of women who would work at making their marriages happy.

The actual wedding ceremony was to be performed by

a longtime family friend, an Anglican bishop. It would take place in the old ballroom, which could easily accommodate the guests. The reception was being held in the Great Hall in the main compound. Ironically the Great Hall had been erected for his late father's wedding to the beautiful Charlotte Sheffield, the current Lady Vandenberg.

Sasha had met his mother many times over the years when she was socializing in Sydney or Melbourne and always returned home saying what a "lovely person" Lady Vandenberg was. She had even suggested Lady Vandenberg might be sent an invitation to the wedding; the twins had met her, as well, and found her "fabulous." But as ever, Sasha's efforts at reconciling mother and son had met with total failure. As far as he was concerned, marriage meant one mate forever. Even the *brolgas* that danced on the river flats knew all about that.

When he went downstairs, showered and changed, he found the women setting out wedding gifts in what the family called the Sistine Chapel. It was really the original drawing room in the east wing, a very large room, cedar-paneled. A bit dark and dingy now, but it had a remarkable plaster ceiling that his father had had restored by a master painter and then insured for many thousands of dollars.

Mountford surveyed the room carefully. The furniture, also high Victorian, had been rearranged for the occasion, and he'd had the station's carpenters make long trestle tables to line three sides of the room. Sasha had hunted up the most beautiful of the old lace-appliquéd linen tablecloths to cover them, and they skimmed the parquet floor. The trestles groaned with their magnificent freight of wedding gifts. It all meant a lot of extra work, but Annabel had been determined that her guests be able to see and enjoy all the lovely things she and Michael had been given.

He called a greeting, acknowledged with sweet smiles, and Annabel ran to him eagerly. "What do you think, Mont?"

He realized his approval was important to his sister, so he backed off into the double doorway, making a frame with his hands.

"Splendid!" he announced. "A marvelous display. Not too many people make the gesture these days. The Austins didn't, remember?"

"A pity, but the custom is disappearing. Too much work, I suppose," Annabel thrust her hand through her short blond curls. "It was Roishin's idea to create all the different levels, and she wants to use those big white porcelain swans for a table decoration."

"Very effective." He let his eyes rest on Roishin's face, marveling that it could appear both sensual and wonderfully tender. "What sort of flowers would you use?"

"Perhaps sprays of white Singapore orchids if I could get them. A little greenery."

"Why don't you get on to the fellow who's doing all the floral arrangements?" he suggested. "I'm sure he could run to a few more orchids." All the flower arrangements and bouquets were being flown in from Melbourne, along with the country's most fashionable floral designer and his assistants. Whatever it took, he would see that Roishin had her porcelain swans carrying masses of white orchids on their backs. "All practice for your own wedding, Roishin," he added lightly.

"Roishin hasn't got any wedding plans," Vanessa told him, glancing at her friend with a smile. "But she could have her pick of at least a dozen eligible men."

Roishin shook her head, obviously wishing Vanessa hadn't said it, but he finished for his sister, "Drawn like moths to the flame!" Idly he moved down the line, reading the cards attached to the wedding gifts. There was tableware of every make, design and color, quietly elegant, which he preferred, or richly embellished. Limoges, Lenox, Wedgwood, Royal Doulton, Royal Copenhagen, Mikasa. Crystal galore, Waterford patterns, Baccarat champagne flutes, wine, sherry, liqueur glasses, brandy balloons. A magnificent ruby decanter and a dozen matching goblets decorated with gold. Silver of all kinds, wine carafes, tureens, trays, an antique silver tea service, candlesticks and candelabra by the score. There were antique clocks, Lalique vases, ceramic vases and paintings. Furniture in one corner—six antique dining chairs, an embroidered screen, a very beautiful French *secretaire* that had belonged to his grandmother for as long as he could remember. Linen occupied the entire length of one trestle, from tablecloths to napkins, through bath towels to satin-bound blankets and the finest American-cotton sheets. All in all, there was just about everything a very fortunate and popular young woman could desire.

He transferred his attention to the sections of wall above

the cedar paneling. "I don't know why someone didn't point this out. The room needs freshening up."

"We weren't going to use it, remember?" Sasha said, looking up. "Besides, you've spent so much already, Mont."

"A coat of paint should do it." Roishin came to stand near him, her particular fragrance entering his nostrils. "What about a lovely blue, instead of the ivory? The same blue as the plasterwork in the ceiling. And maybe we could take that gorgeous Persian rug out of the library just for the occasion. The guests won't be going in there, and the rug has such marvelous rich blues, pinks and reds. Annabel, what about a few gilt-framed mirrors, instead of paintings? There's so much in the attic. Van showed me. Turn on the chandeliers and voilà! It'll look much lighter in mood and tone."

"Why, of course! How delightful!" Annabel exclaimed. "May we have that done, Mont?"

"Whatever you want," he said with gentle indulgence. He ran his hand down her cheek. "I'll have someone mix the paint in the morning. Roishin will have to stand by to ensure it's just the shade she wants. Raid the attic, too, by all means, Roishin. You have carte blanche." He moved toward the door. "I'll be in my study until dinnertime. Call me if there's any lifting to be done."

IN THE MORNING he detailed two of his best maintenance men to take some white interior paint and a couple of tubes of tint from the station store and present themselves to Miss Grant at the homestead for further instructions. He himself had a meeting with one of the big meat buyers flying in from Bahloo Springs, a Mountford property some one thousand kilometers to the northwest. He expected the usual haggling, the disputes about bullock weight, but in the end he almost always got the deal he wanted. Market requirements had changed over the past few years. The smaller three-year-old beasts were in demand, not the larger five- to six-year-old bullocks. He expected he'd sell an entire paddock within the first hour. Southern Cross, crisscrossed by a maze of water channels, was a fattening paradise after the rains. The cattle were in prime condition.

Around midday he returned to the homestead, well pleased with the morning's proceedings. Emily, their part-aboriginal housemaid, was busy polishing up in the gallery, but she called to him that Mrs. M. and the twins were supervising at the Great Hall and Miss Grant was in the east wing with the painters.

He should have been organizing road trains with his overseer; instead, he found himself moving off in the direction of the old drawing room. This course of action was only deepening his involvement, but what the hell! After all, he was expected to approve everything. Roishin Grant didn't need to know his *real* reason for calling in.

As it turned out, she wasn't there, and he felt a stab of keen disappointment. Where was the legendary Mountford independence of heart? Surrendered the first moment she'd dazzled him in that magical dress. She'd probably gone down to the Great Hall where the domed ceiling was being draped with miles of rose and cream tentlike hangings. The framework had taken four of his men the best part of a week to erect, but he'd been assured by the decorator, Sydney's most famous and fussy, that the effect would be sensational. A male assistant had been left behind to stage-manage the job until the decorator returned the day before the wedding to give his all-important okay.

His own men greeted him warmly, as though they hadn't seen him for years. Ernie Powell, known to everyone as Pee Wee, had already moved his gear aside, while Bluey Reynolds, his ginger-haired nephew, was seated up on a plank finishing off a section over the double doorway.

He made a full circuit of the room before he pronounced judgment.

"Nice work, men!"

Pee Wee, who looked like a terrorist but had the mellowest of temperaments, grinned. "Real pleasure, Boss. The young lady had us mixin' away at the color until we got it just right. Celestial blue, ain't it?"

"Damned if I know, Pee Wee, but it's very effective." He glanced at the freshly painted walls, the blue perfectly matched to that of the elaborate ceiling. He could see the Persian rug from the library rolled up at the far end of the room; two matching gilt-framed mirrors with carved flowers at the corners and trails of gold leaves across the top rested against the paneling. Not only that, the enterprising Miss Grant had found a very fancy pair of armchairs, lavishly adorned with gilt scrolls and garlands, which he thought would look fine on either side of the double doorway.

"Looks beaut, don't it, Boss?" the diminutive Bluey called in a voice that would have made a deaf man jump. "Terrific idea Roishin had. A real sweetie, that one! No trouble to paint the place, either. Didn't spill a drop. We're gonna lay the rug and put up the mirrors after lunch. I believe them chairs are to go 'ere." He laid down the roller he'd been using, jerking his thumb vigorously downward. Just at that moment Roishin came back into the room, a charming smile on her face.

It was too much for Bluey, always a disaster around women. Hell-bent on greeting Roishin's return with a flourish, he threw up his hands, the left catching the handle of the roller and sending the tray of paint flying.

There was barely half a second between Roishin's expression changing to that of a woman awaiting something horrendous and the paint cascading all over her.

"You bloody fool, Bluey!" Pee Wee yelled, otherwise frozen in shock, but Mountford had moved in fast, scooping up a cloth from the rung of the ladder and wrapping it around Roishin's hair.

"Don't panic, Roishin," he said in his normal crisp delivery. "Keep your eyes shut and I'll get you under a shower."

She stood perfectly still, her arms folded inward, and he gathered her up, moving to the shower room that served the pool area at the rear of the east wing.

He had the water running within moments. He kept his arms around her, steering them both into the cubicle. She'd started making little breathy sounds and he found himself murmuring encouragement in a voice that seemed to be pulsing with something far stronger than anxiety or concern. As steam billowed all around them, he cupped her face in his hands, holding it up to the wide-nozzled jet. The water-based paint began to thin out rapidly, running in blue rivulets onto the blouse that had born the brunt of the spill. He reasoned the blouse should come off. He loathed the idea of embarrassing her, but it didn't seem the time for false modesty. More paint was coming from her blouse than anywhere else.

"You need to get that blouse off, Roishin," he muttered while the water poured over them like a miniature Niagara. "Don't be embarrassed." He slipped his palm over her collarbone, finding a bra strap.

She seemed to nod her consent, still fearful, apparently, of opening her eyes. He unbuttoned her blouse down the front, peeled it off and threw it outside the cubicle onto the tiled floor. He was totally drenched, which mattered not at all. He continued to direct the water over her with his hands, relieved beyond words that her hair, face and upper body were almost washed free of paint. Now the panic was subsiding, and he started to experience a sense of excitement that was dizzying. Every nerve in his body was humming, every muscle bunched. Her breath was coming fast and he felt her give an involuntary shiver, though steam was swirling around them in clouds.

For one long moment he allowed himself to look at her. How could he not? The strength of her magnetism appalled and confounded him, yet she was beautiful enough to take his breath away. He thought he would remember forever the first sight of her breasts, the upper slopes beaded with water, the rose-colored nipples peaking cleanly against the nearly transparent fabric of her bra. It seemed a fantasy that they should be there together like this. Shock waves were running through him. Pleasure beyond imagining. They were as close as lovers. Body to body. The sinuous slither of the water only acted as a stimulant.

With her eyes closed, head bent, she seemed tremendously vulnerable. She had such graceful shoulders, a swan's neck. Instead of keeping his distance as he'd vowed, he was plunging deeper and deeper into a sensual maelstrom. It came to him that he'd never wanted anything or anyone the way he wanted her. Like it or not, she'd entered his life; now he would never be able to return to his old, cynical self-contained self.

Emotions warred in him, each struggling for supremacy. He wasn't a man to cede control and yet…and yet… He wanted to kiss her, her full tender mouth, the hollow of her throat. He wanted to bend her back over his arm and kiss the white flesh of her breasts. He had to do *something* to assuage the hunger that burned in him so fiercely. She stirred up all the old misery and pain he carried deep within him; she challenged his elemental maleness, but something about her was pure balm. Desire wasn't born out of cold reason but *need*. What he felt for her wasn't just physical.

Slowly she opened her iridescent eyes, staring up at him, surprising God-knew-what expression in his too-intimate gaze. Steam was rising around them like incense, perfumed by the boronia-scented soap that had fallen unheeded to the floor of the cubicle. Her parted lips were trembling slightly. Her slender body seemed to be racked by little tremors.

His hands seemed to be moving of their own accord, driven by a single overwhelming impulse. They skimmed her hips, her narrow waist, shaped the satin-smooth rib cage. Her eyes were still staring into his, brilliantly clear, unaffected by her ordeal, the color now pure green. There was some star in their depths that seemed to be urging him on.

Blood rushed in his ears. He lowered his head abruptly, catching her gasping mouth, sealing it brutally, tasting her sweet breath on his tongue. Her body seemed to melt into his and he tightened his grip on her.

I must have her, he thought. *I* will *have her.* She embodied everything he most feared and worshiped. She set up such longings.

It seemed to go on for a long time, their mouths fused together. He was kissing her as though she were exquisitely delicious and he a famished man. The sweetness of her mouth enslaved him.

David!

Had she moaned it softly? Was she trying to turn her head?

He was infinitely stronger, taller—the top of her head just cleared his shoulder. But whatever happened between them could only happen with her full volition.

He threw his head back almost violently, and it was over. He reached behind her and turned off the faucets, unaware that the silvery glitter of his eyes revealed he was still riding strong emotional currents. Her body was still resting against him as though she was dazed. He had to admit that what had happened *had* been devastating. He dug his fingers through his wet hair, felt it spring back in waves. He stepped outside the cubicle and hunted up towels from a cupboard, then held one out to her. She wrapped it around her like a cloak. She'd been very pale; now color was flooding her cheeks, making her eyes blaze.

"I thought you wanted no part of me?" she asked in a strained voice.

"Oh, come, Roishin! I'm only human." A cool comment to cover what had been a very passionate encounter. "I'll be amazed if you're able to wear that blouse again. We must get you another."

"No need," she said quietly. "I hope you're not going to tear strips off Bluey?"

He shrugged. "Pee Wee's bound to have done that. You must think I'm a hard boss?"

"You've shown a certain hardness to me. I'm not imagining it. It's there."

"Maybe I don't care to see myself one of your potential victims." He gave her a tightly drawn smile. "Now, if you'll wait a moment, I'll send Emily to you. She can bring some dry clothes." After the briefest pause, he added, "I'm sorry that happened, Roishin."

She bound her long dark ribbon of hair around her hand. "Your kissing me or Bluey spilling the paint? I have a feeling it's the former."

"In that case, 'sorry' doesn't cover the situation. At any rate, I'm glad you suffered no harm. I wouldn't have cared to see paint get into your beautiful eyes." He finished pressing a towel over his wet clothing, sopping up the worst of it before he threw the towel over a brass railing. "No need to worry—I won't grab you again. It must have been all that steam!"

She looked at him, a little turbulence in her eyes. "You're speaking from experience here? I understand you've had any number of women friends."

"Not in the shower, no. I do believe that's a first."

She laughed, spilling music in his ears. "Shall I tell Sasha and the twins about the…incident?"

He swung back toward her. "But of course! It'll be the talk of the place, anyway. Better to forget the part where things got out of hand."

"Oh, absolutely!" She coolly matched his tone. "Especially as it's not going to happen again."

Chapter Three

THREE DAYS to the wedding, and the homestead began to fill up. The bridegroom, Michael, and his parents arrived, along with his sister, Carey, and his older brother, Skip, who was to be best man. Red Mountford—David Mountford's uncle—piloted his own plane in from their central Queensland property, Sapphire Downs, bringing his wife, Emma, the two bridesmaid cousins, Leith and Tiffany, and the madcap member of the family, Matthew, a first-year university student on special leave. The following day, another large Mountford contingent flew in, picking up the three groomsmen from a domestic flight along the way. The day before the wedding, the musicians, the decorator, the floral designer, the large consignment of flowers, the caterers and food were scheduled to arrive midmorning by charter flight from Sydney. Several VIPs sharing a private Learjet arrived late that afternoon.

Over the years, the homestead had extended its original ten bedrooms to sixteen to accommodate guests. Most guests would have their own bathrooms; a few would have to share. Temporary facilities had been set up elsewhere in the main compound and the station staff would stay there, vacating their dormitories and bungalows so they could be taken over by guests. A celebration barbecue was being held for the staff, to start immediately after the wedding ceremony, and the station aborigines had planned a special corroboree in honor of the bride and groom on the eve of the wedding.

Excitement was building at a tremendous rate, affecting everyone on the station. A lot of staff had been taken off their normal duties to help out where required—the homestead, the grounds, the Great Hall, which was barely recognizable draped as it was with rippling fabric.

"It's been an enormous amount of work," Sasha admitted to her stepson, "but well worth it, don't you think, darling?"

"Sure." Mountford lowered his coal black head to smile at her. "I just hope to God it all stays in place. Just how much fabric is there?"

"Enough to carpet Monaco," Vanessa joked. "Belle wants sunset, she gets it!" Sunset was Annabel's theme. It was the time of day she loved most. The vaulted ceiling of the Great Hall billowed with pleats of rose and cream interspersed with bands of gold. Ceiling-high poles, bound by more of the rose-colored fabric, had been erected around the perimeter to deepen the illusion of a great tent. It all created a very romantic roseate glow.

Even the actual ceremony in the ballroom had been timed exactly for the moment when the glory of the sky would invade the large room through its arched walls of glass. Afterward the wedding party and the guests would walk across to the Great Hall for a formal sit-down dinner. Dozens of tall glass cylinders were already in place, rising four feet above the table and capped by three-branch candelabra, which in turn held tall pink candles. The floral arrangements that were to go around the bases of the candelabra would be placed there on the morning of the wedding, along with the low display that would run the length of the great table. In keeping with Annabel's sunset theme, the four bridesmaids' beautiful shot-silk gowns were the muted colors of the sky as the scarlet blaze softened into rose pink, mellow gold, misty mauve ombréd with blue and Roishin's rich champagne, which had the faintest shimmer of green. The men's vests had been matched to the bridesmaids' gowns, as were the gold-patterned cravats. The flowers, spiked with lots of bridal white, were to continue the theme.

He would be at the official table of course. Without their father, he was to give Annabel away, so he'd be seated next to her at the reception. He would act also as master of ceremonies. The official table had been arranged at the head of the T-shaped formation, allowing their guests to see them. Sasha and the twins had completed the handwritten place cards weeks ago. They would be given to the caterers to set on the morning of the wedding. There were lots of people involved and things had to run smoothly. Even so, it was going to be a crush. But Southern Cross had hosted many a gala event—balls, New Year's parties, banquets, post-polo parties. No big wedding, though, not since his father's disastrous first marriage. His father and Sasha had been married very quietly in Sydney.

Sasha must have picked up on his thoughts. "Belle's starting to get the jitters," she said. "The big day is closing in. I was a total mess before my wedding. I knew two things. Your father, Mont, had been crazy about your mother, and I was as different from her as it was possible to be."

"You're a very sweet lady, Sasha." Mountford caught her to him and dropped a kiss on her soft springy curls. "You made Dad happy. He loved you. So do I. That's another two things."

"If only your father were here now."

"Listen, Mum, Dad will be watching," Vanessa exclaimed emotionally.

He put an arm around both of them. "He'd be very proud of his girls." His words must have held comfort because they both relaxed. "Now, if Belle's getting nervous, we have to be strong for her. Where's Roishin, by the way?" he added as though it were an afterthought.

"Now there *is* a sweet girl!" Sasha said with obvious affection. "She's been an enormous help to us. Such a pleasure to have in the house. She has the happy knack of mixing easily with everyone. Family and staff."

"Everyone except *you,* Mont!" Vanessa gave him an almost painful dig in the ribs. "Although that must have been pretty provocative stuff, the two of you taking a shower. Roishin is so alluring and you'd be a hard guy to resist."

"You think so?" he said derisively.

"Brother, I *know* so. You nearly crackle with energy and excitement."

"Dear God!" he said.

"You're not in the least vain, are you?" Sasha smiled. "You're the best son a mother could have."

A sense of anger and loss bore down on him abruptly. "So sad my mother never thought so."

"Darling, you were a perfect son to *me*. And you never did hear her side of the story."

"Actions speak louder than words, Sasha," he muttered. "So, then, where's Roishin?"

"I told her to go off and enjoy herself," Sasha said. "We've asked far too much of her, but she's so competent and willing. Last time I saw her, young Matthew was chasing after her."

"You forgot to mention he's already got a crush on her," Vanessa groaned.

"I hope he's not planning on making a nuisance of himself."

"Roishin can take care of herself," Vanessa laughed. "She's used to guys mooning after her."

"No one guy?" As soon as the words were out, he regretted the slip.

Vanessa looked at him keenly. "Why, exactly, do you want to know, big brother? You're interested in her, aren't you? Well, you two would make a terrific team, don't you think?"

"I'd think it would be a case of history repeating itself." It was a bitter remark, but he couldn't control it.

"I understand your feelings, Mont," Vanessa said

simply, "but Roishin's beauty isn't just on the surface. She's a fine human being. Can't you see that? You're usually so fair-minded, too."

He put his arm around her as if in apology. "Be that as it may, Van, there's no getting away from it. Beauty exists to hurt."

HE SPENT the afternoon tracking down a notorious brumby stallion that had stolen two of the station's mares. He took Charlie, his best tracker, and two other hands. A short distance out from the Five Mile they found unmistakable signs of the mob—a waterhole with the sand all chopped up by shod and unshod hooves.

"They're here all right, Boss. Too right!" Charlie wheeled his horse around. "We oughtta make a trap."

It didn't take them all that long to assemble what was really a small holding yard with stout branches lashed together. The country around them was defined by a low semicircle of rocks strung out like giant marbles. In the afternoon light the desert landscape was glowing with the brilliance of ocher, against which the white trunks of the desert gums stood out in a curiously three-dimensional effect. As they rode on, a group of red kangaroos bolted before them before bounding back into the tangled wall of tea-tree scrub that worked effectively as an extension of the trap. Properly broken in, brumbies made good work horses, and the stallion was widely reported as a big, sleek, high-mettled beast.

Less than fifteen minutes later, they came upon the mob.

The stallion led the way on what appeared to be a pleasure stroll. The mares and yearlings followed, with a few foals bunched up at the rear. About ten in all. It was time to close in on them. A stab of pity always hit Mountford at this moment. These were wild ones. They had never known bridle, saddle or hobbles. They would fight for their freedom, especially the stallion, who in no time at all seemed to sense their presence and galvanized himself for action. Mountford saw him throw his head high, snorting furiously, openly defiant of all comers and protective of his mares, two of which he'd taken from right under their noses.

Mountford and Charlie veered off to left and right, forming a rough semicircle with the other two men. He fully expected the stallion to sense the danger that lay ahead, but for once the wily animal was caught unawares. He raced straight for the entrance to the trap, mane and tail flying like pennants, his brood following him, including the foals who were running as fast as their legs could carry them. At one point the stallion broke free, and Mountford roared at Charlie to cut him off.

After that, they stayed right on the horses until the entire mob thundered into the holding yard. The mares stood shivering, giving shrill whistlelike whinnies of terror as they protected their foals.

Virtually all creatures of the wild protected their young, he thought bleakly, his mind inevitably turning to his mother's abandonment. He shrugged off the moment's introspection, and loving horses as he did, immediately began to set about calming them. After a while they seemed to listen. All but the roan stallion, who kept dashing himself against the fence.

Freedom. Precious freedom. *We all want it,* he thought.

Sometime later, he left the men to it, working his way back to the homestead. He was thinking about his mother more than he had thought about her in years. Roishin Grant had stirred it all up. She cut, yet lured him to his very heart. Women were beautiful creatures. More powerful than they knew. He wanted her to leave. Badly. Afterward, he could go back to his well-disciplined life. Or at least try to.

He reflected on Sasha's remark that he'd never allowed his mother to give *her* side of the story. He wasn't comfortable with the thought. But what could she possibly say that would exonerate her? She'd left her husband and child for another man. Not even a man she'd bothered to marry. It was only right that his father had been granted custody. His father had never failed him. Nor had he made the mistake of marrying an unsuitable woman again. Station life wasn't for everybody. Especially social butterflies.

Not that he could honestly put Roishin Grant into that category. He had watched her like a hawk, waiting for a revealing word, an action, but she appeared to be everything Vanessa said. She was charming, warm and friendly. She was efficient and methodical, with considerable organizational skills. She coped well with everyone. She was a clever independent young woman.

He was the one who felt threatened. *He* was the one who was losing his usual iron control—something to be avoided at all costs.

About a mile out from the compound, he spotted someone riding toward him on a motorbike. Probably young Matthew. He loved riding the bikes. Closer in, he saw it was one of the twins. At that distance he couldn't tell which. He started down the slope with the peculiar intuition it was some sort of alarm. Neither Annabel nor Vanessa would normally chase out here.

They met up in a red cloud of dust. He dismounted and went to help her. It was Vanessa. "What's wrong?"

She spluttered through a dry throat, "Probably nothing. But I thought I'd ride out and tell you. It'll be dark soon, and Roishin and Matthew aren't back."

"Back from where?" he exploded, feeling a pang of agitation.

"Listen, don't get angry," Vanessa appealed to him, putting a hand on his arm. "I don't *think* anything's wrong. They went for a drive, that's all. Carey was going to go with them, only Belle wanted her to do something."

"So where did they go?" he asked, his voice impatient. "Surely Matthew told someone where. He knows the rules, if Roishin doesn't."

Vanessa took off her bandanna and touched it to her perspiring face. "He told Aunt Emma the caves."

"They're pretty damned extensive." The network of caves on Southern Cross was a well-kept secret, as much to preserve them as anything else. "What time did they leave?"

Vanessa brushed a wisp of curl from her eyes. "Hours ago. They took a Jeep—"

"Damn Matt!" he interrupted roughly. "I hope to God he's not set on showing off."

"He is a bit excitable," Vanessa agreed.

"He nearly wrecked a bike the last time he was here."

"You'll locate them, Mont. Of course you will. Tell him off when you find them."

"You have my word on that. If he's managed to get them lost… This isn't a cozy little spread like Sapphire. It's vast dangerous country. Matt knows that."

"So does Roishin," Vanessa said loyally. "She's very sensible, Mont. She won't let Matt do anything stupid."

"Who was driving?" he countered, rubbing his frowning brow.

"Matt, I believe."

"Give me the bike," he said decisively. "I'll drive across country. You ride back to the homestead."

"Good idea!" Vanessa looked enormously relieved. "You'll probably see them coming in. Take it easy, Mont. You're Matt's hero. He…he probably lost track of the time."

He shrugged and walked to the motorbike. "You realize if they've got themselves lost or the Jeep's broken down, we might be stuck for the night?" He made a visible effort to curb his anger.

"You'll find them, Mont, like you find people all the time. You know every inch of Southern Cross, even in the dark. Anyway, Roishin will be fine—she's strangely at home in the wild. But Matt'll be a bundle of nerves!"

He sent the bike careering cross-country with the wind streaming alongside. No sign of them, and sunset was closing in fast. Finally he reached the hill country, riding the length of the ancient stone formations. The tracks from the Jeep's tires were easy to spot, but there was no sign of the vehicle. Where would Matt go? Never a man to panic, Mountford discovered in himself an escalating fear, a lot of it to do with Roishin's safety and frame of mind. Being lost in the never-never with its endless confusions of sand dunes and prehistoric rock formations could fill even the stoutest heart with dread. Something would have to be done about Matthew before his thirst for violent action got him into serious trouble.

At the caves an eerie howling wind was blowing through the ravines like the voices of ancient gods. Some people claimed to find it acutely disturbing, even frightening. Sasha wouldn't come near the place. The howling winds were blowing today, though there was no such wind on the open plain. Used to the phenomenon and generally unperturbed by it, he found himself taking it as some sort of omen.

Matt, outback-born, would know as well as anyone how quickly and completely night fell here—going from hot cobalt skies to inky blackness in a matter of minutes, without any comforting man-made interventions like lighting. All the bushman had to rely on was the moon and stars. The Crux, the Southern Cross after which the station had been named, Sirius, the brightest star in the heavens, Orion, the mighty hunter, Aldebaran, the follower, chasing the Pleiades across the sky. A bushman used the stars just as sea captains had used them to know their ship's position. A vast sea of stars.

A vast empty earth. It could be overwhelming. Humans had a powerful atavistic fear of the dark.

Despite the thrumming heat, he broke into a cold sweat of trepidation. Where the hell were they? He raced the motorbike up dunes and down them, roared it across the plain with its good-season bounty of yellow and white bachelor's buttons. Did anyone really need this kind of scare with a wedding going on? In less than an hour, this brilliantly glowing landscape, where everything was thrown into amazingly sharp focus, would be black and desolate, infinitely vast. Matt had to be some kind of a fool to lead her into an area where, over the long years, travelers had been lost forever.

On impulse he rode toward Mountford's Pillar, an ancient butte that rose like a tombstone from the spinifex plain. At this time of day, it was glowing like a furnace, standing some hundred feet above the rippling desert floor. Matt might have continued on there. Named after the Hon. George Clifford Mountford, their ancestor, it was an important landmark on Southern Cross but too far out for a late-afternoon jaunt. He thought he would go mad if he didn't find them soon—evidence, he realized bleakly, of the depth of his emotions.

Halfway between the caves and the pillar, a call rang across the desert like a high-tempered bell.

"Coo-ee!"

Even with the wind screaming in his ears, he heard it. The sound vibrated deep inside him, filling him with tremendous relief. He knew that voice. He'd know it anywhere. It continued to call, floating across the wavelike sands with exceptional clarity and carrying power. It continued to carol for some minutes, and he headed toward it the way he would a beacon that would lead him out of the labyrinth.

"*Coo-ee...coo-ee...coo-eee!*" The legendary call of distress in the outback.

He thanked God she'd had the sense to use it or Matthew had told her. Why wasn't Matthew calling himself? Mountford was more than ever grateful that he knew the desert as intimately as another man might know his home city. But no city could be so fierce or so challenging. Scorching by day, the desert could be icy by night, even in summer. In the depths of winter, under certain conditions, it could kill. The same sand dunes that burned like furnaces during the day could not retain heat. They reared like frozen pyramids, pointing to a billion timeless stars.

Toward the west, deeper into the desert, he spotted four wild camels. They were probably after the fruit of the quandongs. When the bulls came into season they could be extremely dangerous. He had good reason to know. He'd been forced to shoot one a few years back. At least there was plenty of desert plant food about. Almost a bounty after the rains. He'd learned all about "bush tucker" from his early boyhood. The aborigines knew more about desert plant food than the most eminent botanist; they'd survived for sixty thousand years with bush tucker as a staple diet. It was a long education, learning to recognize which families of foods could be enjoyed and which, though apparently identical, were deadly poisonous.

Birds exploded everywhere. The ever-present flocks of budgerigar, the black cockatoos, the white sulfur-crested, the bronze-wings, the finches. A great wedge-tailed eagle was suspended over him, seemingly motionless in the infinite blue and gold air.

The calls had stopped, but now he recognized the Jeep in the distance. It appeared to be rammed against a solitary desert oak. His heart gave one tremendous painful leap. He swore violently even as he tried to formulate a prayer. Out of the corner of his eye he spotted movement, and he swung the bike toward it, skidding in a cloud of dust. There it was again. A scarred, eroded pile of rubble that had once been a hillock crouched on the stony ground like some fearsome prehistoric monster. Around its base, incongruously, was a thick ruffle of luminous green grasses.

A female figure stood up and started to race in his direction. The search was over. Matthew would never get another chance to take her on a jaunt. His anxiety for the boy contrasted sharply with his anger. He felt so exhausted, his breath coming short in gasps as he waited for her to run toward him. Seen against the savage grandeur of the landscape, she looked incredibly fragile.

Yet she could run! Like a gazelle, she was all grace and smooth coordination, her long dark hair streaming behind her.

On compulsion he left the bike and swiftly covered the ground between them, gathering her body to him.

"David!" she exclaimed. "Thank God!"

Now that he had her safe, he scarcely knew what to do. Kiss her. Question her. Berate her with harsh words. Instead, he continued to press her to his body, where she rested as though she had discovered the source of all strength.

"I knew you'd come."

"Did you? My God! From now on I won't let you out of my sight." He took her shoulders and searched her face. Every exquisite inch of it. Yet he was surprised by her toughness. She had *flown* over the stoniest ground. The Jeep had crashed into a tree, at the very least an unnerving experience, yet her eyes even as they clung to his were clear and calm.

"You're not hurt in any way?"

She shook her head vigorously. "I was lucky."

"And Matt?" His tone was both curt and concerned.

She indicated the eroded rocks. "I have him lying down in the shade. He's concussed. Not badly, I think. He hit his head on the steering wheel. He's broken his arm, as well. I've managed to get it in a splint. I've given him a couple of painkillers."

"You could suffer some delayed shock yourself. How did it happen?" He began to walk away, with Roishin half running to keep up with him.

She caught up remarkably quickly, grabbing his arm and trying to make him stop. "David, listen to me. Matt feels very bad. He was very concerned at your reaction. More so than his father's. He's overcome with guilt and shame. The fact is, we were going along quite nicely before he hit a hidden tree stump. He lost control of the wheel...and the rest you know."

"You mean you smashed into the only other tree in the immediate vicinity?"

She nodded wryly. "As luck would have it, yes. The radiator's been pierced. I took a look after I managed to get Matt away from the Jeep. He was pretty groggy and obviously in pain."

"It seems you're asking me to go easy on him."

She smiled and a little color came into her cheeks. "I'm confident that you will."

Matt tried to stand up as soon as he saw them, but Roishin ran to him and gently pushed him back onto the rug she'd thrown on the rough ground.

Mountford dropped to his knees, quickly making his own examination. "Hell, Matt! When are you going to learn?"

"I'm sorry, Mont. I wouldn't have had this happen for the world. I suddenly realized the time and put on a bit of speed. We hit a stump and the wheel was nearly wrenched from my hand. Roishin's been so good. I almost killed her, but she stayed as cool as a cucumber."

"Not quite!" Roishin smiled and put the back of her hand against Matthew's cheek. "I'm sure I let out a yell."

"And who could blame you?" Mountford took a closer look at a couple of tiny butterfly clips she'd used on a gash near Matthew's right temple. All station vehicles carried first-aid kits, and she'd made good use of the contents. A gauze bandage secured the neat splint she'd arranged on Matthew's left arm.

"Damn it. Damn it. Damn it!" Matt was muttering softly. "You must think I'm an awful fool, Mont."

"I guess so." But he smiled and Matthew's expression became more comfortable. "How's the pain?"

"Not so bad," Matthew said stoically. "Roishin gave me painkillers. I really think she should have something herself, even if it's only a cup of tea. It all happened so damned quickly. We'd been having a marvelous time."

"Really?" He shook his head, both relieved and exasperated. "I'm glad Vanessa thought to fill me in on your plans. I'll go take a look at the Jeep."

It was out of commission, just as Roishin had said. No rescue mission could be mounted now. What he had to do was get them to Angel Springs before the light died. They could camp there overnight. There was water, shelter, food. After the rains, Angel Springs, formed by an underflow from a major water channel, became more than a watering hole. It was an oasis with a good supply of desert fruit from the surrounding vegetation.

Everything that was useful he hunted up quickly, loading it onto the bike. He glanced at Roishin who had moved smartly to help him. "I should take Matt first, but I don't like leaving you."

She gave him a competent smile. "I'll be perfectly all right, David. Go now. I'll stay put until you return."

Matthew, when he heard, shook his head gallantly, preparing to give place to Roishin. "Women and children first, Mont."

"Listen, I'm in charge here," Mountford declared.

"Let's put that to a show of hands," Roishin said wryly. At her surprising tongue-in-cheek remark Matthew grinned. "Mutiny, by God! You should know, Roishin, that one of Mont's most marked characteristics is having people do exactly as he says."

The two of them laughed, obviously in sympathy, and Mountford said with extreme patience, "Stop kidding around, you two. We're wasting time. There may be objections to this operation, but I don't see too many options."

"I'll be okay, Mont," Matthew assured him, pale beneath his healthy tan.

"Well, you're tough, as I've discovered." He put a hand on his cousin's shoulder. "In all probability you'll have everyone laughing about this at the wedding. Nonetheless, I'm taking you first. Roishin, if you'll get hold of that rope, we'll strap Matt to me. It'll give him extra support."

It was easier than he'd first expected. Even injured, Matt had excellent balance. They reached the oasis without incident. Secluded behind a ring of willowy acacias, spreading desert oaks and a stand of bauhinias with their radiant white butterfly flowers, the long winding pool was clear and deep, the water good to drink. He settled Matt beneath the canopy. A breeze was blowing, and it was getting much cooler now.

"No foraging for food while I'm gone, Matt. Stay put."

"Right, Mont. I'm so sorry about everything."

"Serves you right for driving so damned recklessly. And don't tell me you weren't."

"It'll never happen again, Mont."

"Well, life's all about learning," he said with a tolerance that surprised even him.

He returned to the Honda and kicked the starter pedal. The engine fired and he roared off, the snarl of the bike shaking out a great flock of little white corellas that decorated the grotesque skeleton of a ghost gum. When he reached the crash site, Roishin was still sitting there, waiting. She seemed to be contemplating the sunset, which had faded from its early bold splendor to the luminescent pastels Annabel had tried to copy for her bridesmaids' dresses.

He parked the bike and moved toward her, extraordinarily edgy, perturbed by all the things that were happening to him. He couldn't get this woman out of his mind. He longed for her, even though there was no place for her in his ordered world. Normally he kept himself on the tightest of rein, but her aura encircled him, growing stronger, more taut. Having to fight it made him moody and dangerous.

"Matthew okay?" She looked neither weary not panicked, an enchanting serenity transparent in her face.

He nodded. "You weren't nervous?"

"What's there to be nervous about? I've been admiring nature in the wild. The light out here has the most incredible crystalline quality. The colors change dramatically all through the day." She took the hand he extended, rising gracefully to her feet.

He wanted to pull her close. He wanted to bend his head and kiss her mouth. Instead, he released her abruptly, stepping back. "So you'd be happy to stay in the wilderness?"

She laughed and brushed off her hands. "I don't think you'd catch me doing that. Not alone. Not yet. But I have a…a *feeling* of belonging." She hesitated, as though reluctant for a moment to put it into words. "It's like hearing music so beautiful it reduces me to tears."

He looked back toward her face, then off to the middle distance. If it was true for her, it was true for him. He felt, however briefly, a sense of absolute communication, one that he was unable—or unwilling—to acknowledge. "Well, your musicality is apparent," he said in a near-dismissive tone. "Who told you to start up the *coo-ees?* Matt, I suppose?"

"No." She seemed surprised. "Matt needed a little time to come around. He took the brunt of the impact. You forget I've spent time on Southern Cross. I know the traditional bushman's call."

He was determined to resist her pull. "Good for you," he said crisply. "They led me to you. I could have wasted another half hour trying to track you down. You've got the best damned *coo-ee* I've ever heard."

"Can I quote you on that?" There was a dancing light of mischief in her eyes.

"Of course." Despite himself he smiled.

"Well, thank you, David. So I'm not hopelessly unsuited to your domain, after all?"

A few taut seconds ticked by as they stared at one another. Did she know his abrasiveness was merely a disguise for the way he was feeling? He frowned and turned away. "Not after today." He glanced up at the sky, which had faded to an incandescent blue shot through with burnt orange. "Ever been on a motorbike before?" He began to move swiftly toward it.

"Have I ever!" She almost had to run, but she managed to keep pace with him. "I have a friend with a Harley-Davidson. It's his prized possession."

"Okay, so you know what to do."

"May I put my arms around you?" she teased.

He looked down on her alluring face. "Stop trying to provoke me, Roishin."

"What an exciting thought! Do you mind if I borrow your bandanna?"

"Not at all." He untied the red scarf around his neck and passed it to her, watching while she tied back her swirling hair.

Like their morning gallop, the ride to the camp brought them exhilaratingly close. When they dismounted, it took an actual force of will for him not to encircle her narrow waist and swing her off her feet. While he scouted up food, Roishin built a fire. By the time he got back, the billy was boiling and Matthew was busy scoffing down shortbread biscuits with some well-sugared tea. It took an enormous weight off Mountford to know that they were coping well. He walked toward the golden circle of light, pouring his haul onto the rug.

"You've found all this?" Roishin asked incredulously.

He went down on his haunches. "Contrary to what most people believe, the desert is teeming with bush tucker. How do you think the aborigines survived? You'll find these red berries delicious. They're full of vitamin C. More so, in fact, than an orange. The mulga apples are quite pleasant, as well."

"Mont's an authority on all this stuff," Matt said, beginning to munch on a desert apple. "A few years back he rescued a couple of English tourists who ran out of water only a few miles from the station's northwestern border. Kept 'em alive on bush tucker. They thought he was sent by God."

"And why not?" Roishin said simply, popping a few berries into her mouth. "You're right! These are lovely— sweet, with a little tang."

"You'll make a real bushie out of her yet, Mont," Matthew grinned. "A lot of people don't take to the wilderness like you have, Roishin. Some go into a real panic. They're frightened of snakes, lizards, those huge goannas, scorpions, feral boars, wild camels. You name it. Mostly they're frightened of the *spirit* of the place. The vastness and the silence. They find it too threatening. And, in a way, *this* place is the scariest of all—and the most beautiful. The Mountfords have stations all over, as you know, but there's nowhere like Southern Cross. This is what Mont calls the beating heart. Our ancestral home."

"I understand why you love it," Roishin said. "Its sheer size, its grandeur. It's not like anywhere else." She gave a sigh of contentment and tilted back her head. "The stars are coming out. Aren't they marvelous? Nothing between us and them."

"There'll be no moon tonight," Mountford warned her. "Just the light from the camp fire."

"Shall I scream, David?" she asked airily. "Just so I won't disappoint you?"

"You won't throw Mountford off balance," Matt said with a roguish grin. "Women never do."

"Is he hostile toward women?"

"I've never noticed it," Matt laughed dryly. "Mont's been voted one of the sexiest men in the country, haven't you heard?"

"Shut up, Matt," Mountford said quietly.

"I did see the magazine." Roishin gave Mountford a charming smile. "Let me get you some tea, David. There should even be a shortbread biscuit if Matt hasn't wolfed the lot."

"Not me, sweetheart." Matt did his best Bogart voice and pushed what was left of the packet of biscuits onto the rug. "There's a slab of chocolate, as well, Mont."

"How's the pain?" Mountford asked, accepting a steaming mug of billy tea from Roishin.

"Hurts like hell, but I'll survive."

"That's the right attitude, Matt. Never give in. Maybe before you turn in for the night, we'll try you with a weak brandy to help you sleep. I'll be off at first light. It'll mean leaving you on your own for a few hours, but I should meet up with the rescue party about halfway."

Nothing, he observed, seemed to disconcert Roishin or shake her calm. Even when the lonely howls of the dingoes broke the silence, she seemed to find the sound just another facet of the desert environment. In the pleasant warming glow from the fire it was easy to tell stories about Southern Cross, stories of station life—the funny, the interesting, the tragic. It was a surprisingly companionable time and the hours slipped by.

Eventually he got Matt more painkillers and sometime

later mixed him a weak brandy from the Jeep's flask. He had brought the Jeep's swag and a rug, and Roishin made Matt comfortable, her manner competent and comforting. Like an older sister. She settled him in his makeshift bed on the silvery white sand. It was thick and springy, not packed hard like the red sand around the claypans.

Mountford built up the fire for warmth, and it wasn't long before Matt drifted off.

Roishin checked on him and caught Mountford's eye. "Let's hope he sleeps. He must be in quite a bit of pain."

He nodded his agreement. "Matt's tough. But he has to stop taking risks. I'll bet he took you bouncing across the scrub. It simplifies matters if you try to keep to the recognized tracks. The spinifex clumps are massive after the rains, and you might expect the occasional hidden stump. The particular area where you were driving is full of hazards. You were lucky."

"Yes, I know. We both had some frightening moments when Matt lost control of the wheel. He didn't panic, though. He kept his head."

"As did you. You've behaved very coolly."

"Women *are* capable, David." She lay back on the rug, looking up at the brilliantly blossoming stars. "The night sky out here is enthralling. It must be the pure air. I've never seen so many stars. Billions of them! They're so big and bright…" She gestured toward the sky. "Tell me about them, David."

Suddenly he felt utterly relaxed. He eased his tall frame back. "The night sky is the subject for innumerable aboriginal myths and legends. There are thousands of them associated with the moon and stars. Strangely enough, the moon is the man and the sun is the woman. Birth and death are always associated with Meenka, the moon man. If a woman wishes to become pregnant, she stares up at the moon. If she doesn't want a child, she's careful not to do any moon-gazing. Aboriginal children are taught that the moon is dangerous. It doesn't like to be stared at."

"I hope the stars don't feel the same way. The Southern Cross is outstanding tonight."

He nodded and put his hands behind his head. "It always is over the station. The desert nomads believe the constellation is the footprint of the great wedge-tailed eagle. The stars of the cross, Alpha and Beta Centauri, are great ancestor figures. The Scorpio constellation originated as two lovers who broke tribal law. Orion spends most of his time making illicit advances to the Seven Sisters, the Pleiades. The Milky Way is the sea of light every spirit must travel to find its way home."

"I'd like to be married under the desert stars," she said.

"Then you'd better marry me."

"Is that a proposal, David?"

"Not to be taken seriously. For both our sakes."

"Why do you say that?" She moved when he hadn't expected her to, propping herself on one elbow and staring down at him.

"You're an exceedingly dangerous woman."

"You *want* to believe that," she accused him.

"I do."

"Can't you tell me why?"

He reached up to release his bandanna from her long hair. It fanned out immediately, spilling around her face and shoulders.

"Women like you know how to make a man suffer." His voice had dropped to a soft growl, and his fingers of their own accord encircled her slender neck.

"What are you trying to do to me, David?" she asked simply. She seemed so very direct and honest. "Are you trying to strangle me with my own hair?"

He tugged on a thick strand until her face was poised directly above his. "You have the most beautiful mouth."

She stared back at him with intensity. "There's such a contrast between what you *say* and what you *do!* It's very, very odd."

He laughed gently. "I'll tell you something odder. I want to make love to you. It's a good thing Matt's on the other side of the fire."

"You're taking it for granted I'd let you?" she challenged.

"You wouldn't?"

"You're very sure of yourself, aren't you, David Mountford?"

"This is something I can't help."

The firelight flickered on her lovely face, revealing a certain inner turmoil. "And you're finding it intolerable? This…attraction you feel?"

The tips of his fingers traced her jawline. "No woman is going to rule my life. I like to be in control." Easy enough to say even though his desire for her was a furious white flame. Some of it must have shown in his eyes, because she trembled visibly. "Come down here, Roishin, and relax. I'm not going to touch you."

"I think you'd do anything when the mood's on you."

"Never by force."

"Why would you need it?" she asked almost bleakly. "After all, you can have any woman you want."

"I want *you*," he said wryly. "And it's making my life hell."

His words seemed to hurt her, shot through as they were with self-derision and hostility.

"David, what you're saying doesn't make sense…" Her voice trailed off helplessly.

"As a matter of fact, it does. To me."

"Has it got something to do with your background? Your past?"

"Let's look at the stars, Roishin. I'm not going to lie here being psychoanalyzed." With a single movement he had her down beside him. A mistake. A flood of electricity flowed from her slender body to his. It was anguish. It was unbearable. It was madness and he didn't give a damn. "Stay here with me. It's warmer."

"My God, David!"

He moved his head so his mouth could graze her cheek. "I want to hold you in my arms." He sighed heavily. "I must be falling to pieces."

"There's a chink in your armor."

"A lot of good it'll do you, Roishin." He spoke sarcastically, but the blood was surging in his veins. "Have you ever cheated on a man?"

"I've never lived with one or told one I loved him, so the answer's no. But you, on the other hand—I've been told you've never been short of girlfriends. You must have broken quite a few hearts."

"If I have, it doesn't make me feel good. But what's to be done, Roishin? I'm a man like any other. I enjoy women. Their strength and their wisdom. I like to talk to them. I don't think I've deliberately hurt anyone. What more could you want?"

"Are you telling me you've never been in love?"

"You've just figured it out?" he asked acidly.

"You must have been a tragic child."

"How touching of you to think so."

"My mother is a divorce lawyer. Did you know that?"

"I've heard it mentioned," he said dryly, turning his head so he could gaze at her profile.

"She encounters a lot of grief in the family courts. Human beings are capable of doing tremendous damage to one another. Love turns to hate, or love and hate coexist. The most damage is done to the children. They suffer dreadfully from marriage breakups. Mostly the pain stays with them all their lives. As for the parents, there can be degrees of guilt on both sides. My mother has been discussing her cases with me for years now. Not the worst ones, the truly ugly ones, when I was younger, but I know a good deal about the subject. My own area is litigation, as you know. That can be fairly distressing at times, but nothing touches the family courts for trauma."

"Roishin, you're not telling me anything I don't know." He spoke with cool precision.

"Of course not. You've experienced it all firsthand."

He felt like a tinderbox about to explode, but he kept his tone cold. "I told you I've put the past behind me."

"I don't think that's true, David. A famous writer once said something like, 'The past isn't dead; it isn't even past.'"

"Brilliant!"

"Don't be angry." She gave him a gentle pleading look.

"That's a tall order, Roishin. I'm not about to bare my soul or disclose any long-buried secrets, if that's what you're after."

"Actually I was thinking more of myself," she said mildly. "You don't deny a certain attraction, yet you're battling an aversion to my physical type."

"You could be right." He answered with extreme irony.

"The other thing is, I've met your mother."

"What?" The word shot out with such a hard ring he turned his head to check that he hadn't disturbed Matt. He hadn't.

"It's a small world," Roishin was saying quietly. "Lady Vandenberg, as well as being the wife of an important man, is an important person in her own right. She's served with my mother on several committees. In fact, they've become quite friendly. I've met Lady Vandenberg many times."

"How very interesting," he drawled, aware that his expression was cold and tight. "How come Annabel or Van have never told me?"

"They know your views on the subject. I understand your mother's name is never mentioned."

"And you find that shocking?" he asked in an attacking voice. "Are you quite sure you understand what happened, counselor, or are you putting *me* on trial? My mother left Southern Cross twenty-four years ago of her own free will. There was a huge scandal that devastated my father and upset the whole Mountford clan. My mother's conduct was shameful, impossible to condone. She broke her marriage vows and she abandoned her only child. That's *my* finding. If she finally found happiness with Eric Vandenberg, well and good. I want no part of her, and I especially don't want to hear what a wonderful person she is now. So far as I'm concerned, charity begins at home."

She studied the stars in silence, then she said, "You're very bitter, David."

"So I am." He answered more mildly. "Aren't the facts good enough, lady lawyer?"

Her iridescent eyes turned toward him. "I sympathize, David. Didn't I convey that?"

"Then who are you acting for?"

"You," she breathed. "Bitterness doesn't heal wounds, David. It leaves them open and festering."

It was a 'judgment' he'd made himself, even as his emotions held sway. "So what are you saying I should do?" he asked harshly.

"End the torment. Your mother speaks of you all the time, David. To this day she agonizes about you."

"Roishin, you're breaking my heart."

She propped herself up again, looking as though she wanted to reach out for him but didn't dare. "Couldn't you meet with her?"

"No," he said in a hard emphatic voice.

"As an adult you've never heard her side of the story."

"I heard it all from my father. I had absolute trust in him."

"He was unhappy and hurting, David. He was a man of considerable power and influence, and your mother damaged his pride. Doesn't it bother you that she may have a different story to tell? She tried very hard to contact you after your father died."

The tension that had gathered in his body found expression in his voice. It sounded daunting even to his own ears. "It seems to me, Roishin, that you've decided to act on my mother's behalf."

"No, David," she protested, the movement of her head making her hair swirl around her shoulders. "It's your antagonism to *me* that's caused me to speak. I felt it rush for me the moment you laid eyes on me that first day—when I was coming down the stairs. It shocked me so much it nearly stopped my heart. It was all there in your eyes. They're wonderful eyes, David, but their expression more often than not *threatens* me."

"Stop this, Roishin. Right now."

She shook her head. "Please hear me out. I know you'd never hurt me. You're a civilized man. The women in your family adore you. What I'm talking about is more an assault on my psyche."

"Dear me!" There was a wealth of mockery in his tone.

"I don't want you to hate me, David. I don't want that at all. And I refuse to be a victim. Your victim."

"Shut up, Roishin," he said very coolly.

"And if I refuse?" She kept her voice steady, but there was a throb of emotion in her eyes.

"Look, you can argue in a thousand different ways. I'm sure you're very good, but the fact remains. I have no mother. I haven't had one for the past twenty years and more. I have a stepmother of whom I'm very fond. I have twin sisters I love. None is the sort of woman who hurts people. Annabel is getting married in a couple of days. She'll be a great wife and mother, a man's best companion. So will Van when her turn comes. As for you, I'm sure you'll make a brilliant marriage. You have everything going for you. You're beautiful, clever, you have the right connections. You're everything a man could want. Every man but me. So much for our wedding beneath the eternal desert stars!"

"I'm not sorry I spoke."

Was there the glimmer of tears in her beautiful eyes? It affected him powerfully. "And I'm not sorry for *this,* either!"

He caught her face between his strong fingers, bearing her down to him, turning her on her back. He caught her mouth beneath his own, burning with a furious frightening passion. Her mouth still bore the taste and scent of wild berries, and he explored it hungrily, mercilessly, the way a bee devours nectar. He could feel her slender body trembling as it had on their other brief encounter. He wanted her. Completely. He wanted everything she was.

It was a love that could destroy him.

Love!

It was over almost as swiftly as it had begun. He sprang to his feet while she lay back. She didn't speak. While he loomed over her, she closed her eyes.

What am I doing? he thought. *I'm punishing her because she's brought me face-to-face with myself. I've searched for her all my life and now I've found her, I treat her abominably.*

What the hell's the matter with me?

God, wasn't it clear enough?

He loved her. He had loved her at first sight.

Another Mountford tragedy to play out?

Chapter Four

HE CAME INSTANTLY AWAKE as the first lambent blue light stole through the desert oaks and moved over the still water hole in long silver wisps. He felt no hint of tiredness, though he had barely closed his eyes. He made a quick inspection of the campsite, his gaze lingering on Roishin's sleeping form. He stretched his limbs briefly, then rose to check on Matt. Matt's face bore a faint grimace as though pain was seeping into his subconscious. The sooner he got his young cousin back to the homestead, the better. Matt's condition meant a quick trip to Derby Base Hospital.

He moved back toward Roishin. Through his fragmented dreams, his mind had been full of her. She had entered his bloodstream and he didn't know what to do about it. He approached her very quietly, going down on his knees.

She was lying on her back, one arm upstretched, the other at her side. Her thick gleaming hair made a dark halo around her face. His eyes fell to her breasts. They rose and fell gently with every quiet breath. Seen asleep, her beauty had an innocence and purity that struck at his heart. It touched him with reverence, longing and—inevitably—passion. His hard body began to stir. Wanting her was coming close to physical torture. He saw that as his punishment. He continued to stare at her, fascinated. His hand moved involuntarily, touched her cheek. Her skin was like satin, lustrous, smooth, warm to the touch. Very gently, he said her name; despite himself, he touched a palm to the curve of her breast.

Immediately she opened her eyes. Her lips moved; her breath fluttered. She arched her back, then sat up with swift sinuous grace, moving almost into his arms.

"It's all right, David. I'm awake." She said it sweetly, as though ready and anxious to help and sustain him.

They were so very close he could see a pulse begin to beat at the base of her throat. He touched a finger to it, let it linger there and felt her heartbeat. His hands began to shape her delicate shoulders, then he pulled her into him, profoundly aroused.

"I don't have the strength to resist you," he muttered.

With one arm, he encircled her, bringing her even closer to him. Her mouth opened under his, her full lips so tender, so soft, surrendering to his mouth's hard pressure with startling sweetness and ardor. The moment would live in his memory, no matter what happened. She had spoken about wounds. She was healing his one by one. It was part of her power. All at once he felt it was time to be brutally honest with himself. Could he trust her? *Could* he trust her? He knew that if he let her go, he would miss her all the rest of his life.

His breathing harsh, he released her. She, too, was quiet, as though she found it difficult to speak. "What is it you want from me, David?" she whispered finally, looking up at his dark head bowed over hers.

It was obvious that she had no certainty in her heart. Why would she? He had shown her a bewildering range of emotions, from outright hostility to blind passion.

"Nothing. Everything," he answered, as if such a contradiction was perfectly normal.

"Oh, David!" Her blue-green eyes turned liquid, sparkled like jewels.

"I think we'd better stand up." He brought them to their feet, keeping an arm around her—it was so damned difficult to let her go. "Come on. Let's walk to the bike. It'll be light soon. The bike will wake Matt if the birds don't. They're starting to call."

"You do expect a search party to be out?"

"You can count on it," he reassured her. "I should meet them halfway. Matt will need more painkillers when he gets up. Make him a cup of tea."

"I'll do that," she said quietly.

"You've done very well."

"I sense that you're still waiting for me to stumble."

"That's the dilemma, Roishin." His dilemma. The contradictions of his heart.

THE HOUSEHOLD didn't settle down again until Rex Mountford flew back into Southern Cross, a chastened Matthew in tow. He'd flown his son to Derby Base

Hospital, and now Matt's left arm was in plaster and a stitch had been inserted in the gash over his left eye. It had been a long worrying night for everyone. As Mountford had predicted, the search party left the main compound in the predawn, meeting up with him several miles from the caves. No one was the least surprised that Mountford had found them, but anxiety had mounted when it became apparent he hadn't been able to make the return journey by Jeep.

An unexpected fallout of the misadventure was that Annabel had had a tiff with Michael. For several hours the wedding appeared to be in jeopardy.

"What started it, for God's sake?" Mountford asked Sasha with some irritation.

"It's not serious, Mont. Really." Sasha gave a feeble laugh. "Michael wanted to go out after you, and Annabel told him not to be a fool. Ordinarily she wouldn't have said such a thing, but she was so worried that Matt might have done something foolish and she'd let Roishin go with him. Poor old Michael was mortified, so it sort of went on from there. Poor boy—he meant well, but he doesn't know the bush at all. He'd only have lost himself."

"You can say that again!" Mountford agreed. "But it's unlike Belle to be so volatile."

"It's a big thing, getting married, Mont," Sasha said, obviously thinking of her own wedding day. "A big commitment. Putting one's life and happiness into another person's hands is pretty scary. Lots of brides *and* grooms get cold feet. It's only a passing thing with Belle."

"That's good to know," he said dryly.

"You know what I mean, darling. Belle loves her Michael. He's a fine young man with a future. He wants to go into politics, I believe."

"I guess someone's got to do it."

"Don't tease, darling. And don't worry about Belle. Anxiety put her under undue pressure. She's extremely fond of Roishin. She and Van were blaming themselves dreadfully."

"I can understand that," he answered crisply. "Well, I hope the lovebirds make it up very soon. We'll have three hundred guests on Southern Cross in another forty-eight hours, all of them expecting to enjoy a wedding."

"And they will, Mont." Sasha looked up at him with myopic intensity. "This will all blow over, you'll see. Why, Roishin's having a good long talk with Belle right now. She's marvelous at calming people down. I suppose it's her legal training. I'm such a ditherer. Roishin will make some lucky man a wonderful wife."

Roishin some lucky man's *wife!* The thought appalled him. For the first time in his life he felt a great wave of sexual jealousy. He didn't take kindly to the idea of Roishin in any other man's arms, much less married to him.

"Is everything okay, Mont?" Sasha was asking in a worried voice.

"Sure." He smiled at her.

"You do look so…formidable at times."

"I'll try to smile more often."

"You should, darling. You have a devastating smile. The sort that makes women go weak in the knees."

He groaned and heaved himself to his feet. "Sasha, I have to be going."

"Your turn will come, darling," she taunted him smilingly. "A man like you only falls once. *Very hard!*"

He didn't answer, but threw her a quick mocking smile.

THE DAY BEFORE the wedding was sheer pandemonium. The airstrip might have been a domestic terminal with all the comings and goings. All the station Jeeps were in use, ferrying people up to the house; even the station helicopter was put into commission, landing quantities of food and the huge consignment of flowers on the rear lawn close to the kitchens and the refrigerated room that would serve as storage. Annabel and Michael were mercifully back on the best of terms, but Vanessa was more upset than she was letting on. She was going to miss her twin, Mountford thought with sympathy. They'd been inseparable from birth.

In the ballroom, where everything was in place save for the flowers, which would be arranged the following morning, the decorator and the floral designer had a serious falling out. The decorator, in particular, was flouncing around like an actor, and Mountford stood in the doorway, for once at a loss. The floral designer, a slim dapper man in informal but expensive gear, suddenly burst into tears. Mountford looked on in horror. Where were the women? He didn't want to get involved in this.

Like a miracle, Roishin and Vanessa appeared in the

hallway, talking earnestly, and he put up a hand to alert them. Both young women jumped to attention.

"What is it, Mont?"

"Listen—a crisis."

"You go, Roishin," Vanessa begged as they took in the situation. "I have complete confidence in your ability to avert a war."

Even Roishin looked a little wary, but she headed for the ballroom.

"There must be some way we can thank Roishin," Vanessa said. "She's been a tower of strength."

"I'll think of something," Mountford promised, grateful himself for Roishin's communication skills. "Personally I'd like to knock those two fellows' heads together. I'm paying them a fortune. They're supposed to be top people, and I expect professionalism. Which includes good sense and good humor."

"They're nervous like the rest of us, Mont. They take their jobs very seriously and they don't like their territory invaded. You have to admit the room looks magnificent!"

"It does." His gaze swept the double-height ballroom with its balustraded gallery—projecting balconies that encircled the ballroom. The musicians would take up their positions there. He could see the gleaming ebony lid of the Steinway already up. Guests would be accommodated along the minstrel gallery, as well as on the terrazzo floor. His eyes returned to Roishin, who was chatting to the two temperamental decorators. "Good grief, will you look at that!" he said softly. "She's got them laughing."

"She really knows how to put on the charm," Vanessa smiled. "I'm glad you recognize she's a very dear and valued friend of this family."

"Whatever you say, Van."

"She's waited a long time to meet you."

"So?"

"So…I figure she's a great success."

"Okay, Van," he said equably, "you want me to say I'm madly in love with her?"

"If ever a man's capable of being madly in love, *you* are."

"What the hell does that mean?"

Vanessa didn't smile. She looked at him very seriously. "You're that rare thing, Mont. You're a man of action *and* imagination. You're strong—like tempered steel—and you're sensitive. You're tough and you're romantic. The right woman could really get to you."

"I haven't cracked yet, Van."

"You will."

They both watched as Roishin made her way back to them. She was wearing burgundy-colored slacks with a matching silk singlet that left her arms and neck bare. A bright turquoise belt was around her narrow waist; there were gold earrings on her ears, gold bangles at her wrist. A casual enough outfit, yet she made it look haute couture.

She moved beautifully, he thought—sliding her legs from the thigh like a racehorse. The muscles of his stomach tightened into a hard knot. The great Irish chandeliers, four in all, had been turned on with brilliant effect, and for a split second, as Roishin stepped under the last one, she was all glittering animation. Her long hair gleamed like some dark exotic wood, her magnolia skin glowed, her eyes with their alluring slant were dense with color, more blue than green.

She looked wonderful.

"A penny for your thoughts, Mont," Vanessa whispered.

"I was just wondering how Roishin solved the problem so quickly."

"Incredible!" she crowed. "David Mountford telling fibs!"

The second Roishin rejoined them, Vanessa asked, "So what was wrong?"

"Neither of them was prepared to give an inch to the other. I suggested a soothing cup of tea, which I'll go and organize. Colin wanted the urns filled with orchids. Darren wanted them filled with the wonderful ferns he'd flown in. I suggested the urns on stands be filled with orchids, the ones on the floor with ferns. A simple compromise."

"You mean *that's* what they were arguing about?" Mountford asked in a disbelieving tone.

Roishin nodded mildly. "A legitimate concern. Darren doesn't like the way Colin's tied the bows on the chairs, either. Actually, I think Darren might make them even more attractive. I suggested he have a go, and Annabel will make the final decision."

"So they've had a tough day?"

Roishin laughed. "It's their job, David. They're both creative people. The wedding is a big showcase for their talents."

"Another falling-out like that and the deal's off," Mountford warned.

"Rehearsal at six, Mont," Vanessa called after him. "It won't take long. The corroboree starts at nine. Roishin's never seen one, you know. It should be exciting."

THE REHEARSAL went off smoothly, and afterward a buffet dinner was served in the formal dining room. The house was humming with music and laughter, the conversation ranging over dozens of topics, all pleasant because of the occasion. The women wore pretty dresses; the men wore jackets and ties.

Looking around with satisfaction, Mountford saw the bridesmaids had paired off with their respective partners for the ceremony. It had even been suggested to him very quietly by Sasha that Vanessa had taken a shine to Skip Courtney, Michael's brother and the best man. The family resemblance was very strong. Both young men were fair, blue-eyed, medium tall, with open engaging faces. Both had ready smiles. It would be surprising if Vanessa *didn't* find Skip attractive, Mountford thought. The twins had the same taste in everything from food to men. And Skip appeared to be pulling out all the stops to entertain Vanessa.

Mountford's eyes moved past them to Annabel, in a very pretty dress the color of sunflowers. Her whole aura seemed overlaid with gold. She and Michael were standing arm in arm in conversation with their uncle, Drew Mountford, a federal senator, and Bishop Morcombe, who was to perform the ceremony. Michael must have finished some amusing story that made the others laugh, for Annabel raised her smiling face to him, her whole heart in her eyes.

Let them be happy, he thought. *God grant her a good life.* They were going to miss Annabel's sunny presence in the house.

As for Roishin, it was taking all his effort not to go and seize her up, take her away from the circle of admiring males, including Matt, who was deeper in the throes of his devastating crush. When it was time to move off to the ceremonial grounds, he made his move, his voice clipped and very decisive. "Roishin's with me."

"Who'd want to cross you, Mont?" Matt said with a grin.

"You can lighten your grip now, David," Roishin told him sweetly as they moved out onto the veranda.

He looked down at her, some expression in his eyes causing her skin to flush. "Just so you know I'm not a man to ignore."

"That, David, is a positive understatement," she answered.

Tonight on Annabel's wedding eve, Meenka the moon man held sway in the sky. He lit up the desert, drawing out all the fiery sun-baked ochers from the ancient landscape, washing it with radiant white light. Around him to the horizon glittered the attendant stars. They blossomed like water lilies, their aboriginal symbol. According to myth, when the moon man had been on earth, he'd been a great lover of women. Meenka had always featured largely in the cycle of life, the affairs of men and women. He would feature in tonight's corroboree.

Only the wedding party and a sprinkling of family had been invited to the ceremony. When they reached the dancing grounds, the didgeridoo boomed out a deep pulsing welcome. Mountford was greeted formally by Charlie Eaglehawk. Mountford, in turn, brought forward the promised bride and groom, who were presented with a splendid bark painting by the tribe's finest artist.

Greetings exchanged, Mountford and the promised couple moved back behind the wide circle of sacred fires, their smoke scented with special timbers. A big circle had been cleared in the sand, then smoothed over. The circle was defined by a ring of glittering gibbers that gave off a strange glowing light as if they were phosphorescent.

Only men took part in the dancing. Women, the musicians, sat in the shadows with their tap sticks and possum-skin drums, and the bound rolls of tree bark they used to rhythmically pound the ground. The dancers had oiled and painted themselves; they wore elaborate headdresses of white cockatoo feathers, and their wrists and ankles were wrapped with the spent feathers of smaller birds.

Mountford looked swiftly around, checking on his party. They were all seated on the rugs they'd brought with them for the occasion. Only Roishin remained standing beside him. Her face looked dazzled. When he touched her shoulder, he felt the shivers of fascination that ran through her body. The scene was riveting, powerful and primeval. It belonged perfectly to the wild desert heart.

For almost an hour, they were part of a ritual as old as time. The quality of the dancing and the mime was extraordinary. The undulating chanting of the women had scarcely less impact. All through the ceremony the women continued to beat the drums with their thin long-fingered hands until, together with the rhythmic tapping of the clap sticks, the sound became hypnotic and curiously stirring. The performance was tender and triumphant in turn, passionate to the point of erotic, in keeping with the strong love magic and the intimacy of the subject. Marriage.

Once when Roishin gave a soft involuntary shudder, he took off his jacket and slipped it around her shoulders, his hand brushing against her beautiful breasts. He wanted to cup them, take their tender weight. His thumbs ached to excite the sensitive nipples.

God help him if the dance didn't stop!

She touched his arm. He found himself linking her slender fingers with his, holding her hand tightly. It was an admission. He knew that. In such a short time she had transformed his whole world.

Yet hadn't his father felt overwhelming desire for his beautiful Charlotte? Passion of this order could be the beginning of great pain. His very soul cried out for her, but why should the depth of his feeling be reciprocated? Why would she, such a beautiful and gifted young woman, be any more suited to the loneliness and isolation of station life than his own mother? Boredom had driven his mother into a disastrous love affair that had wrecked their lives.

History could not be allowed to repeat itself. Unlike

his father, he lacked the capacity to turn the other cheek. He wouldn't sit idly by if his wife spurned him. He knew he had within himself the potential for ruthless action. For vengeance.

Chapter Five

SOME THIRTY MINUTES before the ceremony was to begin, Mountford presented himself outside the bridesmaids' dressing room.

At his knock, his cousin Tiffany, a dark honey blonde, came to the door looking resplendent in her gown of mauve shot with blue. A matching coronet, embroidered, beaded and beribboned with a medieval look about it, completed the outfit. He looked briefly over her shoulder, saw the other bridesmaids scattered around like so many roses in full bloom. The light gleamed on their magical dresses. The whole atmosphere of the room was redolent of perfume, romance and excitement.

"Talk about knock-'em-dead handsome!" Tiffany went up on her toes to kiss him full on the mouth, something she'd been doing since she'd turned sixteen. "If ever a guy can wear formal gear, it's you, Mont. Boutonniere and all!"

"Thanks, Tiffany," he said wryly. "You haven't left lipstick all over me, I hope?"

"Only the normal amount." She grinned. "Just kidding, Mont."

"You look ravishing!"

She closed her eyes. "Oh, God, Mont, do you *mean* that?"

"I certainly do."

Vanessa, a vision of soft beauty in her rose pink gown, hurried over. "I love that silver gray vest and cravat."

"Whatever you do, don't tell me it matches my eyes." That had been Sasha's first comment.

"I'll only think it." She smiled.

"May I come in for a moment, Van? I have a little memento for all the bridesmaids."

"Why do you have to be my *cousin?*" Tiffany moaned.

"You've done so much already, Mont!" Vanessa, used to Tiffany's antics, ignored her.

"It's only a commemorative thing, Van, and it will give me great pleasure."

"Girls," Tiffany called over her shoulder, "gather round."

He set the box he was carrying on a table. Four smaller boxes were inside, all bearing a well-known jeweler's crest. He had commissioned these items many months ago and was pleased with the results.

He presented a box to each of the four smiling women. Three blondes and one with gleaming dark hair sliding down her back. With the small presents went a kiss on the cheek, which the irrepressible Tiffany professed to enjoy immensely.

"Mont, how beautiful!" Vanessa said with a delighted cry that was taken up by the other bridesmaids. She held a commemorative pin of the Southern Cross constellation to the light. Fashioned in eighteen-carat gold, the points of the constellation were represented by precious stones. Diamonds formed the upright of the cross, a ruby to the east, an emerald to the west, a sapphire for the smaller star tucked in under the cross beam.

"I hope you can find someplace to pin them. Annabel's gifts are exquisite." They were already around the bridesmaids' necks—circlets of fine-quality pearls with the clasps sitting perfectly in the hollow of their throats. Each clasp was a large semiprecious stone chosen to enhance their dresses. A garnet for Vanessa, a topaz for Roishin, a tourmaline for Leith and an amethyst for Tiffany.

Now, pins in hand, the four made a rush for the full-length mirrors that had been set around the room.

Mountford made a move toward Roishin, acting on the strongest compulsion. She looked up at him with stars in her eyes. "This is lovely, David. I'll treasure it all my life."

As I'll treasure the sight of you. Her beauty dazzled him like a shaft of sunlight. Where was all his precious hard-won detachment? He felt like a stranger to himself.

"Pin it on for me," she invited, and passed the small adornment to him.

He noticed Vanessa pinning hers to her headdress, but he caught the band of Roishin's low curving neckline midway between her shoulder and the cleft between her breasts.

"I think here." His fingers touched her warm skin. Desire came rushing at him like a great wave. An exquisite scent, half floral perfume, half her own essence, tantalized his nostrils. "You should be painted in that dress." He turned her so she was facing the mirror, his own tall frame reflected behind her.

"'Shall I compare thee to a summer's day,'" he recited, holding his voice to a light sardonic tone. Unaccountably he saw attached to her gleaming coronet a *veil*. A traditional bridal veil. It fell to the floor and stood out around her in a cloud of finest tulle. An illusion, of course, created by his imagination and the quality of the light.

"David, what is it?" she asked hesitantly.

"Nothing," he said dismissively. His vision had overwhelmed him, but he knew better than to tell her what he'd seen, what he felt. The French had a term for it, as they had a term for everything. *Coup de foudre*. A lightning bolt. It had struck him with relentless force.

When he turned around, Sasha was in the room for her final inspection of the bridesmaids. She murmured aloud with pleasure, announcing that they looked as if they'd stepped from a medieval garden. Vanessa pointed to the jeweled pin in her coronet.

"I know, darling. Aren't they lovely? Mont is so thoughtful." Sasha was looking exceptionally chic herself in a stunning two-piece suit with a fitted jacket and a long straight skirt. The color was her favorite powder blue, and she was wearing a magnificent diamond-and-sapphire brooch with matching earrings, very valuable family jewelry Mountford had seen only rarely.

Sasha's small fingers fluttered. She made minute adjustments, primping a billowing sleeve here, twitching the opulent folds of a skirt there.

"We'll have to scoot back to Belle, Mum," Vanessa reminded her.

"Bye, bye, my angels!" Sasha called. "This is one of the happiest days of my life." She blinked back tears. "A little bit sad, too."

LATE AFTERNOON saw them all gathered in the ballroom, which had drawn gasps of pleasure and admiration from family and guests. Sasha had taken her place. Bishop Morcombe, Michael and his attendants were in position.

Mountford looked down at his stepsister's small beloved face. Love *was* a bloom on a woman. An illumination. Annabel looked radiant, though her blue eyes glistened with suppressed tears. Because of her small stature—she was barely five foot three—she wore a short flaring veil attached to a pearl-and-gold crown that gave her height and reflected the design on the embroidered bodice, long sleeves and hemline of her beautiful silk gown. The bridal bouquet had been scaled so as not to overwhelm her, but the flowers in it were many. Roses abounded, extraordinarily beautiful, as were the floral arrangements that had been placed all around the ballroom. He had to admit Colin and Darren had been worth every penny.

"Be happy, Belle," he murmured. "This is your big day."

She swallowed what was obviously a lump in her throat and gave him a melting smile.

The entrance music began and Annabel took his right arm. They began their slow procession with the bridesmaids walking behind them in pairs, Vanessa and Roishin, Leith and Tiffany. As many weddings as Mountford had attended over the years, as many times as he'd been best man, this wedding was very, very special. The first in the family. Everyone had expected he himself would marry long before this, that he, the elder, the brother, would be the first. He saw now his prized bachelor state hadn't been a question of not getting involved. No woman had moved him. Until Roishin. No other woman ever would. Not like this. She had possessed him from the very first moment. Did she know it? She was highly intelligent, intuitive. She knew that his curious attitude to her revolved around an old tragedy. She had made him think about his mother. She had created fleeting confusions about his parents' marriage. About the whole business.

He had to decide how to respond.

When Bishop Morcombe asked the traditional question, "Who gives this woman to this man?", he pressed his thumb against his sister's soft palm, offering her in an unspoken gesture his love and support. For life. Whatever life held in store for his sisters, they knew they could always count on him.

A full two minutes into the ceremony, with Sasha beside him trying unsuccessfully not to cry, the sunset came pouring through the soaring casements in such a rich tide of color it embellished everything it touched. Audible gasps of delight rippled around the room, as though the visitation of the sunset was a most significant and happy omen. A few feet away from Mountford, Annabel smiled ecstatically. He touched Sasha's hand, looked into her dissolving eyes. At that moment, too, he remembered his father. Neither could he escape a momentary vision of his mother, a memory of the two of them standing side by side.

Mountford lifted his head and glanced around the gallery. Every face looked serious and intent, acknowledging this as one of the greatest, most crucial and emotional moments in life. When he married, there would be no mother of the groom for him. No father. No parents. Only Sasha, who had shown herself to be a woman of great heart. He remembered he hadn't wanted his father to remarry, but Sasha had won him over. It hadn't been easy, because he'd been a wildly unsettled child. Barely a year later the twins had arrived. Amazingly he had loved them. They had become a family.

THE USE OF THE GREAT HALL for the reception was an extravagant success. In the words of one guest, it looked like "a grand romantic fantasy," which was exactly what Annabel had wanted. Guests gazed around in open-mouthed delight. With the floral arrangements all in place and the candelabra glowing, the billowy ceiling hangings were shown off to magnificent effect.

"You certainly know how to do things!" Trish Wright, the best-known society columnist, told them during the receiving line.

The bridal dinner, chosen by Annabel, was a feast of

flavors, skillfully presented and served. Honey-glazed duck or roast sirloin of beef followed cornets of trout or breasts of quail on wild rice. The main course came with a variety of vegetables. There were a number of desserts, including Michael's favorites—soufflés, luscious tortes, strawberry shortcakes, chocolate-truffle tarts, all arranged on a fifty-foot-long dessert table dominated by a four-tier wedding cake, a work of art in itself.

When it came time for Mountford to open the speeches, he kept his short. He didn't need any notes. He knew what he wanted to say. From the looks on the faces turned to him he realized his simple words had struck a solemn chord, so he ended with a funny story about Annabel when she was growing up. The hall broke into laughter and he immediately proposed a toast to the health and happiness of the bride and groom.

May they live happily ever after, he thought. *I want them to be happy.* Above all, now at this moment, he wanted to be happy himself. It was time for him to catch hold of his life. Live it. He'd struggled too long with a burden.

IT WAS SEVERAL DAYS before the household could settle to anything resembling normal routines. Annabel's wedding had been a great ceremony, marking a turning point in family life, and everyone felt deflated. Though she tried her best, Vanessa couldn't hide the intensity of her feelings. She had lost her other half. The bond between the twins had been so very, very close that some of the life seemed to go out of Vanessa as she strove to make the adjustment.

"It'll take time," Sasha confided to Mountford, "because of how close they were. Annabel, happy as she is, will feel the separation, too. You know what they were like, Mont. When Annabel hurt herself, Vanessa cried."

At the family's request, Roishin had stayed on a few extra days, but it was time for her to return to her own world. "Why not let Van go back to Sydney with Roishin?" Mountford suggested. "For that matter, you could go, too, Sasha. Both of you need a little company right now. I have to admit there's a certain melancholy in the air."

And so it was arranged.

But what about him? He was a man and he was expected to manage on his own. For the first time in his life, he had doubts about his ability to do so. He'd become very used to having Roishin in his home. Her hold on him, no matter how short the time had been, was profound. Yet he had decided not to speak. Not yet.

She had come to Southern Cross for a vast celebration—hardly a typical experience of life in the outback. Annabel's wedding had been a brilliant and memorable occasion. "There's never been a wedding like it!" Trish Wright reported in her newspaper. The homestead had been filled with people. Bright, intelligent, sophisticated people, who had made the house resound with their conversation and laughter. But there were long months at a time when the family scarcely saw a soul. Unless one coped well with isolation, knew how to use one's inner resources, relationships could founder. It had happened before. It could happen again. He might glory in Roishin's beauty and grace, in the ease and delight of her companionship, but what about her needs, her interests? Running Southern Cross and supervising the chain of Mountford pastoral properties was his life. Any woman he married would have to be self-reliant to survive. Often she would be alone. And loneliness was a time bomb waiting to go off.

His thoughts made him so restless Sasha accused him of stalking around like a panther. He just hoped his eyes didn't give out the same wild glitter when they fell on Roishin. He knew she was wary of him at some level. Maybe in love with him, too, but not liking him at all. He wrestled with the whole thing for hours. It wasn't fair to Roishin, he thought. As a child he'd been infinitely betrayed. Why should he blame *her* for that? Just because she was beautiful in his mother's fashion? Yet his fears wouldn't fade.

A sense of loss bore down on him all through that last day. He knew Southern Cross was going to feel overwhelmingly empty. He knew, too, that he was at a pivotal stage in his life. He had to make a move, had to think seriously about marrying. Until he'd met Roishin, he'd considered Cate Sinclair a suitable match. At one time Sasha had taken it upon herself to promote a marriage. Cate was a charming, sensible, station-born young woman. The Sinclairs owned several sheep and cattle properties around Queensland, and he was well aware that Cate's parents would be delighted to have him for a son-in-law. All of them had been invited to the wedding, and he'd danced with Cate, spent some time with her. She'd appeared to savor his company. He liked her. He'd always liked her. Before meeting Roishin, he'd begun to grow fond enough of her to consider the future. Cate was a straightforward person, outback born and bred.

But he didn't love her. Love didn't happen to order. Still, there was safety with Cate. Station life was her world.

It was a shock to find himself in so much inner turmoil. He could never resume his life as if nothing had happened. He couldn't put Roishin Grant behind him. She existed. She had illuminated his life. It was agony to let her go. It was cruel if she felt even a little of the passion that bloomed in him. He was a man on the edge. And he looked it.

Now it was evening, and he sat in the library with Roishin almost quietly for half an hour, then held out his hand. "A walk before bed, I think." In his dreams she lay beside him, his arms capturing her. Sheltering her.

"You're going to have to relax, David," she said. "Sasha's panther analogy isn't half-bad."

"Maybe I'm trying to stave off the hour when you're gone."

"That's no comfort, David." She moved beside him, at his shoulder. "You're in pain because of me. On the one hand you want to forget me totally. On the other, you… rather enjoy having me around."

She was so direct it took him by surprise. "I'm not going to deny it." He clasped her hand without thinking, linking her fingers with his, feeling sensation flood through every layer of his skin.

"You won't *let* me know you," she said.

"Which direction are we walking in?" he asked, the air around them fairly crackling with static.

"I don't really know. I guess I don't care."

"Roishin, stop it. You sound upset."

"The hurt seems to be there. On both sides." She laughed a little and looked up at him. "How can you see in the dark?"

"I'm used to it." He shrugged. "Little by little your eyes will become accustomed to it. For now you can hold on to me."

"I'd like that, David." She tightened her grip. "What are you planning to do when we're gone?"

He didn't even want to think about it. "All manner of things," he said casually. "Running the station is demanding work. I have to take a trip to north Queensland to visit one of our properties. Uncle Rex will be coming along with me and so will Bob Sinclair. Bob's thinking of buying the place."

"Bob Sinclair. That's the distinguished-looking man with iron gray hair and a rather magnificent mustache."

"Come to think of it he's had that as long as I can remember. He was a close friend of my father's."

"And he's Cate's father?"

He gave her a quick glance. Even in the semidark her skin had the luminescence of a pearl. "Why should I find that a leading question, counselor?"

"I understand you and Cate are great friends?"

"I've known her all my life."

"I found her very friendly and charming. Lovely when she smiles. She's a composed and confident young woman."

"Thank you for your approval," he said in a mocking voice.

"She'd make an excellent station wife."

"I'm sure of that." He steered her away from an overhanging branch of white bougainvillea. "Is this conversation going anywhere—or are we wandering in the dark?"

"All our exchanges have an undertone, David. You know that as well as I do. I'm trying to sort a few things out. She's in love with you."

"She's never said as much."

"David, you know she is."

"Would you prefer it if she wasn't?" he asked.

She shook her head. "Why do I make you so quickly hostile?"

"Why do you make me feel things I'm not sure I want to feel?"

"So it's a question of resentment. What kind of woman am I, David? What is it you resent? Please tell me."

They had reached the old summerhouse, a Victorian folly. All around it grew a ravishing old-fashioned pillar rose. By day its petals were the finest velvet crimson; by night it was almost the fabled black rose. Only the rich sumptuous scent remained the same. He drew her inside through the perpetually draped entrance before answering.

"What kind of woman are you? Let's see. My considered opinion is…a witch!" Which was to say everything he loved and feared.

She moved toward the circular cushioned seat, turning her face to the starlight. She didn't smile. "Ironic, when you're so expert at casting your own spells. Let me ask you, David, do you feel a woman like me would find Southern Cross a prison?"

"All these questions, Roishin! Yes, I do. Unlike these roses, you've grown and thrived in a far different environment. I can't emphasize it strongly enough—it's something I've lived with for a very long time. You're used to the excitement and glamour of big-city life. You have a career."

"You don't think I could leave it with ease?"

"*Could* you?" he asked in a dark skeptical voice.

"You sound as though you have doubts."

He stood a little distance from her, looking out over the garden. "Yes, given that I wish to avoid a tragedy."

Her hand flew to her breast as though he had wounded her. "Your mother didn't leave Southern Cross because she found station life intolerable, David."

He actually leaned forward and pulled her to her feet. "How did my mother get into this?" he demanded, his hands on her shoulders.

"Your mother is the problem, isn't she?"

He released her abruptly. "I think we'd better finish this conversation. Your way is to dredge up the past. Mine is to leave it where it belongs."

"Deep in your psyche? Because that's where it is, David. And that's what explains your attitude to me. You demand things from me. A…a passionate involvement, yet you push me away. Not anymore. I'm not going to take your rejection without putting up some sort of fight. This is *my* life, too. Something happened to us that first day."

"Indeed it did! A kind of classic infatuation." The harshness of his tone gave him both pain and pleasure.

"Much, much more!" she said with a spirited lift of her chin. "It could be love, if you'd only let it happen."

"And then?" he challenged her. "We could both pay very heavily. Have you thought of that?"

"David, I'm *me!*" she said in a despairing voice. "Not your mother. *Me!*"

"And you're too damned good to be true!" The hint of anguish goaded and upset him. What was the dark place in him that drove him to hurt her? It was wrong, *wrong,* but he couldn't help it. He caught her in his arms as if he'd never let her go. The thought of her leaving depressed him deeply.

Hunger overpowered him. A driving need of the heart and flesh. It seemed as strong in her, because her whole body trembled, conveying a piercing sweetness and an exhaustion of conflict.

"I love you, David," she said with a depth of feeling that left him humbled and greatly aroused.

Desire burned across his skin. He found her mouth unerringly, engrossed in communicating the passion that flowed through him so turbulently it was purest anguish. He kissed her until she gasped for breath, until she cried his name in a soft frantic moan.

Kissing her wasn't enough. He wanted everything she

was. Heart, mind, the incomparable pleasure of her body. She was simply the most beautiful joyous creature he'd ever seen or dreamed of or envisioned. It would be worth it to have her, no matter what the outcome. At that moment he was prepared to pay the price.

"Do you know I saw you wearing a wedding veil?" he muttered, his mouth against the silky skin of her throat.

"You imagined it." Her answer was shaken and tender.

"It was so real. I swear I saw it that afternoon of Annabel's wedding. I pinned the Southern Cross to your gown and turned you to face the mirror."

"I remember."

"The feeling inside me was so intense. You know, if you married me I'd never let you go."

"You're all I'll ever want, David. Beside you, everything else has no meaning at all."

"And nothing and no one will save you. You must understand that. I'll never let you leave me or take our child."

At last he had articulated his private profound grief. Grief toward the two people he had loved and trusted.

Roishin's head snapped back and she spoke with great seriousness. "We have to address these fears, David. Fears that spring from your childhood. Can't you look for answers from your mother? Great rifts in a family can be many-sided."

He had an eerie sensation that he was being led where he didn't wish to go. "My mother fell in love with another man and went away. That's clear enough. I recognize it affected me, but that was a long time ago."

"I don't think either statement is true, David."

"And you have the right to question me?"

"I don't mean to make you angry, but yes. You've given me that right, whether you're prepared to admit it or not."

"My dearest Roishin," he said in an ironic voice, "what a picture you make among the roses. However, you don't know what you're talking about. So much for the legal training!"

She reached out to him, held his arms. "Your mother denies all charges against her, save one. Your father wanted a large family, yes. So did she. But she *couldn't* have more children."

For an instant he was stunned, almost deprived of speech. "What *is* this, Roishin? I won't listen."

"Please," she implored. "For me. You didn't know?"

"I'm very skeptical indeed of any story you're going to tell me. I've heard nothing about this."

"Not even the miscarriages? She had three in as many years."

He put his hand to his eyes as though shielding himself from a painful sight. "My God, Roishin, I know you believe this, but it's simply not true."

"Your father made no secret of the fact that he wanted a large family. At the very least, three children. It's easy to understand. He had a magnificent home, a huge area of land. He wanted to put his sons on it. He didn't want you to be a lonely only child. Your mother tried desperately— it must have been terrible for her—but she couldn't carry beyond six weeks. It might be hard for a man to understand properly, but words wouldn't encompass a woman's grief, the awful sense of loss and failure. That man, Alex Turner, was in the wrong place at the wrong time. He was sympathetic to your mother. Probably he fell in love with her. Your father was furious, jealous and affronted."

"Ah, so my *father* was the one in the wrong now?" There was anger, shock, disgust in his voice.

"Misery forced your mother out. Your father must have been a hard man on some issues, David. He did his very best to turn you against your mother."

"Isn't it going to be hard to check out her story?" he asked with icy calm.

"The thing is, do you *want* to?"

"It doesn't bother you what the result might be?"

"It's my only hope. Too many emotions rage in you. They've got you in their grip. You question my suitability to become your wife? I couldn't consider it while you feel this way."

"Then forget it," he rasped.

"Tragically, I'll have to," she said quietly. "I'm not going to approach marriage full of trepidation."

"I don't think I'd gotten around to asking," he said brutally.

"I know you can be cruel."

"So be warned. If you've fallen for the great spiel my mother gave you, you've shown no loyalty to me." Even as he said it he felt pain. "How can you be so clever and such a pushover for a sob story?"

Her voice was quiet, but it held great dignity. "What your mother had to say assuredly got through to me, David. But I listened with an open mind. Your tragedy is that you won't!"

Chapter Six

AFTER ABOUT A WEEK, while he tried desperately to absorb himself in the affairs of the station, Mountford felt driven to put through a call to John Morcombe. The bishop had baptized him, as he'd baptized the twins. If John Morcombe knew anything of Roishin's story, he wouldn't lie. Mountford had already sounded out his uncle Rex and drawn a blank. Now as then, the entire Mountford clan fell in with his father's line. One fact did escape: the business about "Charlotte's taking a lover" had never sounded "absolutely right" to Rex. Disturbed, Mountford had made the decision to carry his inquiries further.

Bishop Morcombe was in the depths of far-north Queensland, the deacon told him. It was four more days before Mountford was able to hold his conversation, which again yielded only a little information. Morcombe told him quite straightforwardly that he'd always been "deeply sympathetic to Charlotte's plight." Whatever that might have been. He didn't elaborate even when drawn. The bishop was being very careful. He recalled one occasion when Charlotte had been ill. He had understood at the time that she'd suffered a miscarriage.

The single piece of information struck at Mountford's defenses with tremendous force. When had he stopped believing in his mother? Why? He had a vivid memory of his father calling him into his study, sitting him down in the big leather armchair that dwarfed him, telling him his mother had left them. There had been no attempt to soften the blow. His father had given it to him straight. His mother had formed "a bad friendship" with Alex Turner, the writer, who had been staying on Southern Cross gathering background material for a book. Turner had shown himself to be a scoundrel, a man not to be trusted, although the six-year-old Mountford had quite liked him. Now, suddenly, Turner was a monster, his adored mother a traitor to the Mountfords and the proud Mountford name. All the kisses and hugs and smiles had meant absolutely nothing, he'd learned. His mother preferred a *monster* to him and to his handsome, greatly respected father. He'd decided he would never forgive her defection—something, he now saw, his father had actively encouraged. From that day in the study, he had turned into a difficult child, hiding his wounds in headstrong action. He'd only cast off that image when he went to boarding school, then university, where he'd made quite a name for himself academically and on the sports field. Not many people had divined the ache in his soul, the pain of severance that had never really gone away. Had his wonderful father done *that* to him? If so, it was a dreadful crime. Against him. Against his mother. He had no other option but to go to her and beg for her version of past events. One thing was certain: pitted against his father and the combined strength of the Mountford clan, she wouldn't have stood a chance.

HE HAD NO TROUBLE finding where Roishin lived. He paid the taxi driver, staring up at the large apartment building on Sydney's North Shore. Vanessa had given him the address, obviously agog at what was going on, which he promised to tell her when he called again. Beyond the impressive outline of the building, he could see the sparkling blue of the harbor. Vanessa had told him, too, that Roishin's parents had presented her with her own apartment as a twenty-first birthday present. They must have forked out quite a bit, he thought.

As he reached the entrance, two young women were coming out the security door. They smiled at him and allowed him through even though they should have known better. He had intended to buzz the intercom, but it suited his purpose to surprise Roishin.

When she opened her door to him, her face flooded with color. She was wearing a loose top of violet silk over patterned leggings. A violet ribbon tied back her long hair. She looked as beautiful as ever. Maybe more finely drawn, as though she'd lost weight. As though somewhere inside of her she ached. He wanted her so badly it was a wonder it didn't shine out of his eyes. She hadn't been out of his mind for one second.

"David, how extraordinary!" Her breath caught. "I was thinking of you only this minute."

Her agitation steadied him. "That's nice. May I come in?"

"Of course. Please. Come through to the living room." She led the way to a well-proportioned, highly attractive room with sliding glass doors leading to a plant-filled balcony with views of the magnificent harbor beyond. Her legs in the tights looked incredibly sexy; her high breasts pushed gently against the silk of her loose top.

"Sit down," she invited, indicating a sofa upholstered in a soft coral with a scatter of striking cushions. "Are you in Sydney on business?" She took a seat opposite him, crossing her sleek, thoroughbred legs neatly at the ankle.

Desire ran through his body like a flaming arrow, yet he managed to keep his tone conversational. "*Unfinished* business, yes." He looked around, noting how the grace and charm of her personality was reflected in the way she had decorated the room. There was artwork to transform the walls, sheer draperies at the doors, a tall glass-fronted cabinet with a collection of what looked like antique dolls, books, elegant objects and flowers. Lots of flowers. He would expect that. "I like your apartment."

A luminous smile. "A twenty-first birthday present from my parents. As I'm their only child, they tend to spoil me."

"That would be easy. How have you been?"

"Fine." She paused, moved her graceful shoulders, corrected herself. "No, not really," she admitted. Then, in a little flurry, "David, do you know your eyes actually seem to burn like ice?"

"They've missed looking at you." He sounded almost curt in his intensity.

Even so, her eyes grew misty, jewel-bright between their thick, feathery lashes. "It's worth the agony to hear you say that."

"Was it *that* bad?" Loving her, wanting her, he still couldn't seem to lower his entrenched defences.

"It was agony for me," she said simply, allowing his sardonic tone to slip by her. "Aren't I allowed to say that?"

"Certainly, if you *mean* it."

"I do." She rose in her poised fashion, perhaps stalling for time. "Would you like something. Coffee? I was about to make some."

"I'd rather you sat beside me." He held her gaze when he wanted to hold out his arms. Hell, what was the matter with him? Was he terrified of revealing his own capacity for caring? "I want to talk to you," he said finally.

"And I want to listen."

"So sit down. Why are you so nervous?"

"I always am with you around." A wry smile fanned her mouth. "In fact I go weak at the knees."

"Then sit here." He patted the other cushion on the sofa. "I can see I'll have to cultivate more charm."

"What you've got is more than enough for me." She took her place beside him, an innocent enough action yet powerfully seductive. "What did you want to talk about?"

He obeyed an uncontrollable impulse. He reached out and drew one finger along her cheek. The skin felt like rose petals.

"Important things, Roishin," he said. "I thought you should know, since you're the one who set me free." He paused. "I spent several hours with my mother yesterday."

Her eyes held surprise, joy, a trace of apprehension. "So what happened? Tell me!"

He captured her hand, held it loosely and found it wondrous, the closeness. "It went well. More than well. It was total reconciliation. We parted at peace. For most of my life I've been conducting some sort of war with my own mother. I regret it now. *You* forced me to face the situation. Face myself. Thanks to you, it's over."

The tears that shimmered now brimmed over. "David, I'm glad. So glad! Now the old wounds can heal."

"And you can take credit for being the physician." His voice vibrated with deep feeling. "The extraordinary thing is that after the first few minutes we felt little sense of estrangement. I had my mother back as I'd known her when I was a child. She told me so many things I knew nothing about. Things my father had deliberately kept from me. No one should do that to a child. But I could see how it had all happened. My mother told me she felt that if she'd stayed on at Southern Cross she'd have gone under or even died. She spoke with complete honesty, no bitterness toward my father. She's still very beautiful. She's obviously found happiness with Vandenberg but our reconciliation had real meaning—for both of us. Not that it wasn't painful. At one stage I thought the pain would kill me, but certain things had to be said. Because of my father, my mother was made an outcast. I was supposed to be the center of his world, yet he allowed me to become... twisted."

"David, no!" She leaned for him swiftly, put two

fingers to his lips, sealed them. "I won't let you say that. It's not true. When it comes to the things that matter, you have *heart*. Of course, you're rather good at slamming down the barriers, as well," she added, her eyes dancing wickedly.

"I'm sorry, it's become almost a way of life."

"You have to let someone else in," she suggested. So gently. "I do love you." She gave a shaky little laugh and exultation filled him.

"How will you prove that?" he demanded.

"I could kiss you for a start."

Her whole being seemed to radiate light and love, flooding him with desire that was not without anguish. "Come here to me," he begged, drawing her across him so her head rested back within his encircling arm. "Now, go ahead. Show me how much you love me, because I'm certain I love you even more!"

They were fine words, beautiful words, and they gushed up from some wellspring deep in his heart.

She arched her back, then lifted an arm and locked it around his neck. "This is one of those moments I'll remember all my life. David, I love you. It's like I—"

"Hush!" His control was shot to pieces. What he felt for her was so elemental, so inexorable in its fierce passion, he cut her off abruptly, trying to put everything he felt for her into one single, all-consuming kiss. There was pain in it, and old grief, which miraculously unknotted as her sweet, open mouth flowered and she matched him in ardor.

"I love you," he muttered, feeling that something priceless and beautiful had been given to him. "Life without you would be unimaginable!"

He could feel her body trembling in his arms. Both of them had slid down on the sofa where they lay locked together, limbs entwined. He felt pounded by emotions so great, it was like being caught up on the crest of a great wave. His hands sought her breasts through the soft, sinuous cloth. He could feel her heart pounding. Oh God, how he wanted her! Madly…badly—yet he wanted the exquisite anticipation of their wedding night.

"David!" She sighed, a little lost cry.

He gentled his embrace, forcing himself back to control. They had all the time in the world. He could wait. "I'm here," he murmured tenderly. "No armor. No defenses."

She opened her eyes with their lovely, liquid shimmer. "You need none with me."

"No." He brought his mouth softly back to hers. "Marry me, Roishin. I promise I'll do everything in my power to make you happy."

Her gaze was steadfast. "David, I'm honored. My answer is yes."

This time, the kiss they shared was deep and reverent, promising a lifelong devotion. He cradled her to him. "You're sure you can adapt to station life?"

"I already feel a sense of *belonging,* David. I think that's crucial. And I'll have you as my perfect companion through life."

"Then I'll have to live forever!" He smiled and dropped a kiss on her dark, fragrant hair. "No need to forgo your career, either. Southern Cross will always need a good lawyer. If it's my wife, so much the better."

"You're serious?" She half lifted her head, staring at him with widened eyes.

"Of course I am! You worked hard to acquire your skills. I want you to use them. I want you to have a rich, multi-layered life. Southern Cross is a big enterprise—you might be surprised *how* big. In fact, there's quite a large investment portfolio for you to explore. With your background you're definitely going to be an asset."

"I hope that's not why you're marrying me," she teased.

"What do *you* think?" he asked quietly. It was a wonderful feeling to be able to show the full extent of his love, in his eyes and in his voice.

"I think I love you with all my heart," she answered emotionally. "I think I want us to be married under the desert stars. A vast dome of glittering, floating stars, and the Southern Cross looking down on us. I want our wedding to be so memorable it will endure in our minds forever. Is it possible, David?"

His heart soared. He was filled with a wonderful joy and pride in her. "Not only possible, my darling," he said and his voice rang with promise. "It's going to happen."

There are 24 timeless classics in the Mills & Boon® 100th Birthday Collection

Two of these beautiful stories are out each month. Make sure you collect them all!

If you have missed any of these books, log on to www.millsandboon.co.uk to order your copies online.